Penguin Books

Penguin Modern Stories 9

Penguin Modern Stories 9

Edited by Judith Burnley

Penguin Books

Penguin Books Ltd, Harmondsworth,
Middlesex, England
Penguin Books Australia Ltd, Ringwood,
Victoria, Australia

First published in book form in Great Britain by
Penguin Books Ltd 1971

Made and printed in Great Britain by
C. Nicholls & Company Ltd
Set in Monotype Baskerville

Contents

V. S. Pritchett

Our Wife 7
The Editor Regrets . . . 20

Ruth Fainlight

Soir de Fête 45
The Expatriates 59

Frederick Busch

Something is Moving Just Under the Skin 85
Breathing Trouble 103

Mel Calman

The Fifty Minute Hour 129
The Artist 132

Biographical Notes 141

All these stories are published here for the first time in this country.

V. S. Pritchett

Our Wife

I agree that my wife is a noise and a nuisance, especially in a seaport and in a sailing place like Southampton. Even her little eyes are noisy. People come down to sail at the week-ends, clumping about in gum boots and sweaters and you hear Molly's voice and ridicule by the quay.

'Stupid yachting people. Look at *him*. He's missed the mooring twice. They can't even sail.'

In the restaurant – it is called *The Ship* – it is ten to one she will be shouting and then she'll suddenly stop dead like an astonished child.

'Why does everyone stare?' she says.

'I expect it is because your conversation is more interesting than theirs,' I say.

And Trevor, who is with us, of course, and who always repeats her last phrase or mine, slaps his eager knee and says:

'Yes, more interesting.'

'After all, you *were* talking about my first wife,' I say.

Another slap from Trevor who grins and says: 'Your first wife!'

Molly is as noisy as a pretty guttersnipe. Or as Jack (I remember) once said: 'As a blow lamp.' Jack was her first husband.

The noise is what has attracted us all to her. We have

loved it. She has opinions about everything. She loves an argument. Anything will do. In the old days, I remember, she started a row about whether Jack and I were the same height. He was, in fact, exactly the same height as myself, six feet one and a half inches. She wouldn't have it: the ruler was wrong, she said, and so was the tape measure. We stood in our stocking feet against the wall like two kids who had outgrown their strength, while she went on to argue that all the weights and measures in the shops were fraudulent. That memory of Jack and me standing against the wall, ten years ago, takes me to what he said in a pub in a little place on the Kent coast where they used to live. She was sitting on a bar stool between two men who were arguing with her about sailing – for this she hated more than anything – and Jack and I heard her say to one of them:

'You want cooling down,' and she put her hand out for the ice bucket. If she had been tall enough – she was less than five feet high and short-sighted too – she would have reached it and emptied it over their heads. Jack was ill, as he often was in those days. In the lazy, detached, speculative voice of the very sick, he said:

'See that? Two of them. Molly is a girl who needs two husbands at a time.'

He had seen something I had never noticed, and with a little of the malice of one who was either warning or defining me – even arranging for the succession.

I am a construction engineer and I was working near their village on a new dock for tankers that was being built in this marsh country. I was a widower living in lodgings without much to do in my spare time except play about with my boat. All those attacks on people who sailed were really attacks on me. It was one of the bonds between us – her hatred of my boat. She and Jack lived in an old house in the village that had become a hell of trucks and bulldozers on the way to our dock. I got to know Jack and Molly when a big tree was blown down in a gale into their garden and made a large gash in a brick wall. I talked to them and very soon I was offering to clear up the mess. Molly's husband was not strong enough. He was hacking at the tree with a weak man's fury, and was soon exhausted. I got a machine from the dock and soon they were watching me at work. I am a practical man. I'm good at things like that. The noise of the machine drowned her opinion of what I was doing. All she could do was to shake her brown hair.

In the following evenings, I rebuilt the wall and she stood arguing that it was 'only a theory' that plumb lines hang straight. After that job was done I was captured. It was an old house and soon I was mending doors, unstopping drains, relagging pipes, putting in washers, repairing their car. I even painted a door bright blue after she and Jack quarrelled about the colours. And all the time she was arguing about how our dock would pollute the river, destroy the countryside and drive away the bird life.

'Think of the tankers bringing oil for your car,' I'd say.

Then she would turn on Jack's doctors, on hospitals, and then on Jack and me. ('Men.') Men were always up to something.

'You can't deny it. Look at Jack. Look at you. It's guilt,' she'd say.

And then she'd get on to 'guilt' and say Jack was over-sexed or turn about and say he was under-sexed. Or that he threw money away. Or never spent a penny. Or was shut up in himself. Or perpetually running after other women. She wore her brown hair short in those days and had the habit of giving a nervous sniff in the middle of her sentences – an original and wistful sound in the general clatter which attracted me – and her face would go very red, while her mouth went sputtering gaily away like a little motor bike.

Jack listened to her, blinking busily as if he were taking notes. After a tirade, he'd get up, give a nod and say quietly:

'She's an old character.'

And he would go off, leaving me with her. I would often get up to go with him, but she would stop me.

'Stay here. He's going to sit on the sea wall. Leave him alone. It may be a poem.'

For Jack was a poet; here was the fascination for me. In my trade I'd never run across a poet. Goodness knows how they lived – he read for publishers, I think – but every so often he would go up to his room or sit on the sea wall and, as if he were some industrious hen, he would (as I once said) lay a poem. Molly was angry with me. She allowed no one to make jokes about that, except herself.

I wish I had not made this joke for in a few months his health got very bad. He collapsed. It was I who took him to hospital. I thought he simply had an ulcer. He sat up in bed with a tube in his mouth and I tried to cheer him up.

'You must not make me laugh,' he said. 'It will tear the stitches.'

In a few days he came home, walked down the village street, took a glass of whisky when he got back and that night he died.

The first thing Molly said to me was indignant.

'He borrowed five pounds from me this morning,' she said. Then she became exalted and tender.

'It was wonderful that he left the hospital the day before that nurse who was so good to him was leaving. She couldn't bear the matron. No one could.'

Then her grief overcame her.

'I can't bear it,' she wept. 'I can't believe he isn't upstairs now.'

'Neither can I. I've never felt like this before.' I loved

Jack. I loved her. I had, I felt, been married to both of them.

'The lock on the wardrobe door has gone again,' she suddenly said, angrily weeping and accusing me.

I put my arm round her shoulders. She had become motionless and heavy as lead with grief and she shook my arm off.

'I'll go and look at it,' I said. 'Leave it to me.'

For a poor man Jack had occasional reckless fits. He hankered after expensive antiques. This wardrobe I knew well for I had three or four times tried to repair the lock for them. Owing to the weight of the doors, it was often going wrong. It was a huge oaken piece brought over from France by Huguenots – so Molly swore – in the seventeenth century and it stood in their bedroom. It was the first of Jack's purchases and she and he had a monumental row about it. She had been going to send it back to the shop but Jack saved it in a very clever way: he wrote a poem about it. This made it sacred in her eyes. After this he became a secret furniture buyer and had to store the stuff out of her sight and once or twice I collected it for him.

'So that is what you and Jack were up to,' she said after he died and looked with admiration on our shadiness. To punish me – and Jack too – she sold the lot, but not the wardrobe.

The episode became another bond between us, especially because of the to-ings and fro-ings of the sale, during the time of her grief. Her grief recalled mine when my wife had died and we often talked about it. She would gaze and nod and talk quietly. She became, except for the tiny sniff, a soundless person. Slowly her grief passed. After a year my job at the dock came to an end. I was to be moved to the London office and I started packing. Molly's character suddenly returned to her when she saw my clothes stacked on the table in my lodgings.

'It's a good thing!' she said. 'It will get you away from that idiotic boat.'

My transfer to London was a victory for her opinion. She glittered with victory.

'I'll take you out in it,' I said, 'for a last sail.'

I was astonished, even moved, by her reply:

'All right!' she said defiantly, but I could see that, despite her victory, her lip was trembling. I could see that she did not want me to leave, and I didn't want to leave her. I knew that when we were out on the water and I was, perhaps, coming about and making her duck the boom, I would be able to say what I could not say to her on land. We set off, but soon it began to blow, the sails rapped out and the wind carried away everything she said. She was indignant and frightened. When we got back she said once we got ashore:

'You're a masochist like Jack. It is all guilt.'

'I'm going to sell her,' I said, looking down at the boat from the quay wall. While we were out and I was putting in a reef I had asked her to marry me.

'When you sell it,' she said.

I sold it.

Unluckily for her, we hadn't been married for three months when the firm moved me from London to Southampton. There was the sea again! There were those detested, lovely white tents dotted over the water.

'All yachtsmen are liars,' she said when she saw them accusing me of arranging my transfer. I paid no attention to her; in fact, the trouble we had moving the furniture to our house took her mind off it.

Our house at Southampton was small. I wanted to put the wardrobe – she called it the armoire – on the ground floor; but she said it must go into the bedroom. To get it up there I had to take out a tall window and put a hoist in from an attic. The thing weighed a ton. It took two days and three men to get it into the bedroom. It had been Jack's first extravagance and because of this and his poem Molly was proud of the difficulty it caused. She stood in the garden shouting at the men and came peering at it, to see they did not damage it. In fact the lock did scrape the brickwork when the thing was half way in.

The scrape on the brickwork must have weakened the lock or perhaps the damp summer affected the doors in some way, for they did not easily close. In the winter there would be a sudden click and one door would swing forward. I put it right and then, after a malicious lull, the wardrobe – the armoire I should say – started again. Sometimes I worked on the lock, sometimes I wedged and re-wedged the piece, blaming the slope of the floor.

In the end I succeeded and for a long time the thing was quiet. But one night when I was making love to Molly a door came groaning open like a hound.

'What's that?' said Molly pushing me away.

I paused in my efforts.

'It's only Jack,' I said. 'It's haunted.'

Now why on earth I should have said such an appalling thing and at such a moment, I cannot think. If there is one thing we all know it is that you should never make a joke – if you call that a joke – when one is making love. I would have given anything to take the words back. Perhaps it was an admission that I was beginning to want help, as Jack had done.

The effect on Molly was surprising. She sat up, put on the light and looking excitedly at the doors, she laughed.

'That's very perceptive of you,' she said, admiring me.

I was shocked by her laugh and pushed her down again. But, to be frank, love was a fitful thing with Molly. Now we were married, she said I bullied her into it. She got free of my arms, put on the light once more, gave herself a shake like a dog and gazed in a rapture of importance.

'It's weird,' she said. 'It *could* be haunted. Jack always said nothing is forgotten.'

Molly loved to sit up arguing in the middle of the night until I was exhausted. She said that all things were permeated by the people who had touched them. Now I made my second mistake. I said the armoire was probably alive with the hands of Huguenots. This idea annoyed her.

'It's very funny about you,' she said. 'I didn't know you were a jealous man. Or are you trying to change the subject?'

Jack! Huguenots! All of you! Listen to this. I want help, I cried to myself.

We were still arguing at three o'clock when she changed round and said:

'I'm glad you're not a jealous man. That means a lot to me.'

I was carried away by this compliment and the softness of her voice. Only utter exhaustion could have put me off my guard.

Working in Southampton I could see from my office window the sloping funnels of liners, the cranes dipping towards them; and beyond that the water. As I have said, there was always a sail or two in sight and at weekends there were scores of them. I had sometimes to go to boatyards and there I would look with longing at some craft with beautiful lines on the stocks outside the sheds. The wings of the angry gulls and their quarrelling voices made me think of Molly with love and it was while I was gazing in this weak mood at a beautiful, dark blue twenty-five-foot yawl one afternoon that I saw a man climb out of it. He was a tall, lazy-voiced fellow, with a tired face, very slim and fair.

'She's lovely,' I said.

'Lovely,' he said.

'Cigarette?' I said.

'Cigarette. Thanks,' he said. 'I am selling her.'

'Selling her?' I said.

He nodded. I nodded. An interesting fellow, quiet, a listener. We walked round the boat and had a look inside.

'Frankly,' he said, 'I can't afford her. I've got to give her up. I've just bought an Aston Martin. I can't run both.'

Speed was what he liked, he said. He liked to *move* and he gave a lick to his lip; he was a man like myself, a man giving up one thing for another. I sighed at our singular unity.

'We might do a deal – if I can persuade my wife,' I said.

'Ah,' he said, 'your wife.'

His name was Trevor – I asked him to come up to the house and have a drink.

'But not a word,' I said.

Trevor was an understanding man.

'Who is this man you're bringing up here?' my wife said. 'One of your sailing friends – I know! What are you and he up to?'

'No,' I said. 'He's given up sailing. He can't afford it.'

One more victory was in my wife's small eyes. And when Trevor arrived, wearing a white pullover under his dandyish long jacket, and very narrow trousers, she looked up from one to the other of us to see who was the taller. I saw her immediate interest. Without realizing it, I was at the beginning of a master-stroke. I had brought to the house a man who had given up boats. She was excited by the arrival of an ally.

'My husband's mad about them, quite out of his mind,' she said to Trevor. 'He's thinking of them all the time. He's always up to something, hanging round boat yards – don't think I don't know; he pretends he's at the engineers' – but it's always a boat.'

'A boat,' said Trevor. There was a gentle weary note in his voice and it conveyed to her that mine was one of those infantile and tedious vices that afflict so many men and from which he was now free.

'Better than chasing women,' I said.

'Women!' she said. 'It's a substitute! Don't tell me.'

Trevor listened with appreciation to both of us as we wrangled. He lived alone and from one to the other of us he looked with pleasure at the excitements of home life. My wife, walking up and down and clattering on, with a glass in her hand, was adding to her victories, and Trevor occasionally glanced at me with private congratulation.

'I'll tell you what happened the other night,' she cried. 'We've got an old French armoire in our bedroom and the lock keeps going wrong. He makes out he's repaired it, but I don't know – it's weird! It opens every time we get into bed. Do you know what Tom said? He said "I bet that's my first wife again."'

'Ha, ha, ha,' she laughed. 'Look at his face. Guilt.'

'Guilt it must be,' I said.

'You've been married before?' said Trevor, his only original sentence. I felt a curious gratitude to him for saying this; it created an intimacy.

'Of course he has,' said my wife. 'He keeps quiet about it. That's what is infuriating about him. He keeps so quiet.'

'Jack was quiet,' I said.

'No need to bring up Jack,' she said in her sacred voice.

'Who was Jack?' said Trevor.

'He was my husband,' she said, stopping with dignity. And then she turned on me.

'Tell him about her iron boot,' she jeered.

'Iron boot!' said Trevor. He was overjoyed by her. But she saw she had gone too far and calmed a little.

'Not actually an iron boot,' she laughed and when she laughed her eyebrows were like a pair of wings. 'Her skates. He took her roller-skating – roller-skating, my dear! – and one came off and she fell over and he got engaged. Poor Tom.'

Then Trevor uttered his next original sentence to me.

'Why don't you mend the lock?'

'He's always mending it – or says he is,' she said. 'He's useless with his hands.'

'It's a French thing, very heavy, eighteenth century,' I said.

'Seventeenth,' she said. 'The Huguenots brought it over.'

'Full of Huguenots,' I said.

Trevor heard out this dispute and then he uttered three original sentences.

'My mother has got one,' he said. 'We had a lot of trouble with it. We got it right in the end.'

I gazed at Trevor's hands. Like his voice they were limp and tired. They were long and thin.

'I wish you'd mend ours,' Molly said, in a business-like way.

'And then we'd get some sleep,' she said, with a sharp look at me.

'It's probably like my mother's. They're all alike. I don't mind having a go. Tomorrow?'

I saw that I had found a treasure. The boat was as good as mine, if Trevor and I worked together about it. And there was more to it than the boat.

'There you are!' said Molly, sneering gaily at me, at having an order obeyed as simply as that.

The following evening I found Trevor on a sofa in our

sitting room with a large broken-veined bruise on his forehead. He had mended the lock, but he had moved my wedges; and just as he was testing it, the door swung open and hit him on the head. Molly was mopping the wound.

I elected him at once as Molly's additional husband.

Our life, or rather my life, is more peaceful now: I don't mean less noisy or less quarrelsome, but simply that Trevor now bears some of the burden. He comes round most evenings and if he misses a few days, she is after him to find out what he is up to.

'He has girls in his flat,' she says angrily when she comes back.

'I know! Making out he stays in and listens to records. He never listens to ours!'

'He likes noise. He said so last time when he was here. It's company.'

Trevor turns up again and he and I say nothing about our transaction. She has been out with him in his racing car which terrifies her and to me she says:

'It's nothing but sex. A substitute. You defend him, of course.'

It is true that when he runs her up to London for the day I go sailing. When he brings her back she says:

'Racing drivers are a lot of impotent morons.'

I say to Trevor:

'She's an old character.'

'Character,' says Trevor, slapping his knee at the word. Then, with a sly look at me, for he likes danger as much as I do, he says perhaps:

'Let's go and eat at "The Ship".' (It is at the place where I keep my secret boat.)

We drive down, and at the first sight of a sail she starts about 'the stinking yachtsmen'. At dinner she says in a voice that makes everyone in the restaurant stop eating and stare at us:

'Guilt, that is what it is! There is something going on between you two. Men!'

And when her voice drops for a second, she entrances both of us with that other noise: the little, dog-like sniff.

V. S. Pritchett

The Editor Regrets . . .

Friday afternoon about four o'clock, the week's work done, time to kill: the editor disliked this characterless hour when everyone except his secretary had left the building. Into his briefcase he had slipped some notes for a short talk he was going to give in a cheap London hall, worn by two generations of protest against this injustice or that, before he left by the night plane for Copenhagen. There his real lecture tour would begin and turn into a short holiday. Like a bored card player, he sat shuffling his papers and resented that there was no one except his rude, hardworking secretary to give him a game.

The only company he had in his room – and, in a way, it was a rather moody friend – was his portrait hanging behind him on the wall. He liked cunningly to draw people to say something reassuring about the picture: it was 'terribly good' as the saying is; he wanted to hear them say he lived up to it. There was for him a strange air of rivalry in it. It rather overdid him. There he was, a handsome mixture of sun-burned, satyr-like pagan and shady, zealous Christian saint under the happy storm of white hair. His hair had been grey at thirty; at forty-seven, by a stroke of luck, it was silken white. Its face and his was an actor's, the nose carved for dramatic occasions, the lips for the public platform. It was a face both elated and ravaged by the highest beliefs and doubts. He was energized by meeting it in the morning and, enviously, he said Good-bye to it at nights. Its nights would be less tormented than his own. Now he was leaving it to run the paper in his absence.

'Here are your tickets.' His secretary breezed into the room. 'Copenhagen, Stockholm, Oslo, Berlin, Hamburg, Frankfurt, Munich – the lot,' she said. She was mannerless to the point of being a curiosity.

She stepped away and wobbled her tongue in her cheek. She understood his restless state. She adored him, he drove her mad and she longed for him to go.

'Would you like to know what I've got outside?' she said. She had a malicious streak. 'A lady. A lady from Guatemala. Miss Mendoza. She has got a present for you. She worships you. I said you were busy. Shall I tell her to buzz off?'

The editor was proud of his tolerance in employing a girl so sportive, rude and so familiar; her fair hair was thin and looked harassed, her spotty face set off the knowledge of his own handsomeness in face and behaviour. He liked the state of war between them.

'Guatemala! Of course I must see her!' he exclaimed. 'What *are* you thinking about. We ran three articles on Guatemala. Show her in.'

'It's your funeral,' said the girl and gave a vulgar click to her tongue. The editor was, in her words, 'a sucker' for foreigners; she was reminding him that the world was packed with native girls like herself as well.

All kinds of men and women came to see Macaulay Drood. Politicians who spoke to him as if he were a meeting, quarrelling writers, people with causes, cranks and accusers, even criminals, and the mad: they were opinions to him and he did not often notice what they were like. He knew they studied him and that they would go away boasting 'I saw Macaulay Drood today and he said ...' Still, he had never seen anyone quite like the one who now walked in. At first, because of her tweed hat, he thought she was a man and would have said she had a moustache. She was a stump, as square as a box, with tarry chopped off hair, heavy eyebrows and yellow eyes set in her sallow skin like cut-glass. She looked like some unsexed and obdurate statement about the future – or was it the beginning? – of the human race, long in the body, short in the legs and made of wood. She was wearing on this hot day a thick, bottle-green velvet dress. Indian blood, obviously; he had seen such women in Mexico. She put out a wide hand to him; it could have held a shovel; in fact she was carrying a crumpled brown paper bag.

'Please sit down,' he said. A pair of heavy feet moved her with a surprisingly light skip to a chair. She sat down stiffly then and stared without expression like geography.

'I know you are a very busy man,' she said. 'Thank you for sparing a minute for an unknown person.' She looked formidably unknown.

The words were nothing: but the voice! He had expected Spanish or broken English of some grating kind, but instead he heard the small, whispering bird-like monotone of a shy English child.

'Yes, I *am* very busy,' he said. 'I've got to give a talk in an hour and then I'm off to lecture in Copenhagen ... What can I do for you?'

'Copenhagen!' she said, noting it.

'Yes, yes, yes,' said the editor. 'I'm lecturing on apartheid.'

There are people who listen; there are people upon whom anything said seems not to be heard, but rather to be stamped or printed. She was receiving the impress of the walls, the books, the desk, the carpet, the windows of the room, memorizing every object. At last, like a breathless child, she said: 'In Guatemala I have dreamed of this for years. I've been saying to myself "Even if I could just see the *building* where it all happens!" I didn't dare to think I would be able to *speak* to Macaulay Drood. It is like a dream to me. "If I see him I will tell him," I said, "what this building and what his articles have done for my country." '

'It's a bad building. Too small,' he said. 'We're thinking of selling it.'

'Oh no,' she said. 'I have flown across the ocean to see it. And to thank you.'

The word 'thank' came out like a kiss.

'From Guatemala, to thank *me*?' the editor smiled.

'To thank you from the bottom of our hearts for those articles.' The little voice seemed to sing.

'So people read *The Instigator* in Guatemala,' said the editor, congratulating that country and moving a few papers on to another pile on his desk.

'Only a few,' she said. 'The important few. You have kept us alive in all these dark years. You have held the torch of freedom burning. You have been a beacon of civilization in our darkness.'

The editor sat taller in his chair. Certainly he was vain, but he was a good man: virtue is not often rewarded. A nationalist? Or not? he wondered. He looked at the ceiling where, as usual – for he knew everything – he found the main items of the Guatemalan situation. He ran over them like a tune on the piano. Financial colonialism, he said, foreign monopoly, uprooted peasants, rise of nationalism, the dilemma of the mountain people, the problem of the coast. Bananas.

'It is years since I've eaten one,' he said.

The woman's yellow eyes were not looking at him

directly yet: she was still memorizing the room and her gaze now moved to his portrait. He was dabbling with the figures of the single crop problem when she interrupted him.

'The women of Guatemala,' she said, addressing his portrait, 'will never be able to repay their debt to you.'

'The women?'

He could not remember; was there anything about women in those articles?

'It gave us hope. "Now," I said, "the world will listen,"' she said. 'We are slaves. Man-made laws, the priests, bad traditions hold us down. *We* are the victims of apartheid, too.'

And now she looked directly at him.

'Ah,' said the editor, for interruptions bored him. 'Tell me about that.'

'I know from experience,' said the woman. 'My father was Mexican, my mother was an English governess. I know what she suffered.'

'And what do you *do*?' said the editor. 'I gather you are not married?'

At this sentence, the editor saw that something like a coat of varnish glistened on the woman's wooden face.

'Not after what I saw of my mother's life. There were ten of us. When my father had to go away on business he locked her and all of us in the house. She used to shout for help from the window, but no one did anything. People just came down the street and stood outside and stared and then walked away. She brought us up. She was worn out. When I was fifteen he came home drunk and beat her terribly. She was used to that, but this time she died.'

'What a terrible story. Why didn't she go to the consul – why –'

'He beat her because she had dyed her hair. She had fair

hair and she thought if she dyed her hair black like the other women he went with, he would love her again,' said the childish voice.

'Because she dyed her hair?' said the editor.

The editor never really listened to astonishing stories of private life. They seemed frivolous to him. What happened publicly in the modern world was far more extravagant. So he only half listened to this tale. Quickly, whatever he heard, turned into paragraphs about something else and moved on to general questions. He was wondering if Miss Mendoza had the vote and which party she voted for? Was there an Indian bloc? He looked at his watch. He knew how to appear to listen, to charm, ask a jolly question and then lead his visitors to the door before they knew the interview was over.

'It was a murder,' said the woman complacently.

The editor suddenly woke up to what she was saying.

'But you are telling me she was *murdered*!' he exclaimed.

She nodded. The fact seemed of no further interest to her. She was pleased she had made an impression. She picked up her paper bag and out of it she pulled a tin of biscuits and put it on his desk.

'I have brought you a present,' she said, 'with the gratitude of the women of Guatemala. It is Scottish shortbread. From Guatemala,' she smiled proudly at the oddity of this fact. 'Open it.'

'Shall I open it? Yes. I will. Let me offer you one,' he humoured her.

'No,' she said. 'They are for you.'

Murder. Biscuits, he thought. She is mad.

The editor opened the tin and took out a biscuit and began to nibble. She watched his teeth as he bit; once more she was memorizing what she saw. She was keeping watch. Just as he was going to get up and make a last speech to her, she put out a short arm and pointed to his portrait.

'That is not you,' she pronounced. Having made him eat, she was now in command of him.

'But it is,' he said. 'I think it is very good. Don't you?'

'It is wrong,' she said.

'Oh.' He was offended and that brought out his saintly look.

'There is something missing,' she said. 'Now I have seen you I know what it is.'

She got up.

'Don't go,' said the editor. 'Tell me what you miss. It was in the Academy, you know.'

He was beginning to think now she was a fortune-teller.

'I am a poet,' she said. 'I see vision in you. I see a leader. That picture is the picture of two people, not one. But you are one man. You are a god to us. You understand that apartheid exists for women, too.'

She held out her prophetic hand. The editor switched to his wise, pagan look and his sunny hand held hers.

'May I come to your lecture this evening?' she said. 'I asked your secretary about it.'

'Of course, of course, of course. Yes, yes, yes,' he said, and walked with her to the outer door of the office. There they said Good-bye. He watched her march away slowly, on her thick legs, like troops.

The editor went into his secretary's room. The girl was putting the cover on her typewriter.

'Do you know,' he said, 'that woman's father killed her mother because she dyed her hair?'

'She told me. You copped something there, didn't you? What d'you bet me she doesn't turn up in Copenhagen to-morrow two rows from the front?' the rude girl said.

She was wrong. Miss Mendoza was in the fifth row at Copenhagen. He had not noticed her at the London talk and he certainly had not seen her on the plane; but there she was, looking squat, simple and tarry among the tall fair Danes. The editor had been puzzled to know who she was – for he had a poor visual memory; for him, people's faces merged into the general plain lineaments of the convinced. But he did become aware of her when he got down from the platform and when she stood, well-planted, on the edge of the small circle where his white head was bobbing to people who were asking him questions. She listened, turning her head possessively and critically to each questioner, and then to him, expectantly. She nodded with reproof at the questioner, when he replied. She owned him. Closer and closer she came, into the inner circle. He was aware of a smell like nutmeg. She was beside him. She had a long envelope in her hand. The Chairman was saying to him:

'I think we should take you to the party now.'

Then people went off in three cars. There she was at the party.

'We have arranged for your friend ...' said the host. 'We have arranged for you to sit next to your friend.'

'Which friend?' the editor began. Then he saw her, sitting beside him. The Dane lit a candle before them. Her skin took on, in the editor's surprised eye, the gleam of an idol. He was bored: he liked new women to be beautiful when he was abroad.

'Haven't we met somewhere?' he said. 'Oh yes, I remember. You came to see me. Are you on holiday here?'

'No,' she said. 'I drink at the fount.' He imagined she was taking the waters.

'Fount?' said the editor, turning to others at the table. 'Are there many spas here?' He was no good at metaphors.

He forgot her and was talking to the company. She

said no more during the evening, until she left with the other guests, but he could hear her deep breath beside him.

'I have a present for you,' she said before she went, and gave him the envelope.

'More biscuits?' he said waggishly.

'It is the opening canto of my poem,' she said.

'I'm afraid,' said the editor, 'we rarely publish poetry.'

'It is not for publication. It is dedicated to you.'

And she went off.

'Extraordinary,' said the editor, watching her go, and appealing to his hosts, 'that woman gave me a poem.'

He was put out by their polite, knowing laughter. It often puzzled him when people laughed.

The poem went into his pocket and he forgot it until he got to Stockholm. She was standing at the door of the lecture hall there as he left. He said:

'We seem to be following each other around.'

And to a Minister who was wearing a white tie: 'Do you know Miss Mendoza from Guatemala? She is a poet,' and escaped while they were bowing.

Two days later she was at his lecture in Oslo. She had moved to the front row. He saw her after he had been speaking for a quarter of an hour. He was so irritated that he stumbled over his words. A rogue phrase had jumped into his mind: 'Murdered his wife' – and his voice, always high, went up one more semi-tone and he very nearly told them the story. Some ladies in the audience were propping a cheek on their forefinger as they leaned their heads to regard his profile. She had her hands in her lap. He made a scornful gesture at his audience: he had remembered what was wrong. It had nothing to do with murder: he had simply forgotten to read her poem.

Poets, the editor knew, are remorseless. The one sure

way of getting rid of them was to read their poems at once. They stared at you with pity and contempt as you read and argued with offence when you told them which lines you admired. He decided to face her. After the lecture he went up to her.

'How lucky,' he said. 'I thought you said you were going to Hamburg. Where are you staying? Your poem is on my conscience.'

'Yes?' the small girl's voice said. 'When will you come and see me?'

'I'll ring you up,' he said, drawing back.

'I'm going to hear you in Berlin,' she said with meaning.

The editor considered her: there was a look of magnetized, inhuman committal in her eyes. They were not so much looking at him, as reading him. She knew his future.

Back in the hotel he read the poem. The message was plain. It began:

I have seen the Liberator
The foe of servitude
The god-head.

He read on, skipping two pages, and put out his hand for the telephone. First he heard a childish intake of breath, then the small determined voice. He smiled at the instrument; he told her in a forgiving voice how good the poem was. The breathing became heavy, like the sound of the ocean. She was steaming or flying to him across the Caribbean, across the Atlantic.

'You have understood my theme,' she said. 'Women are history. I am the history of my country.'

She went on and boredom settled on him. His cultivated face turned to stone.

'Yes, yes. I see. Isn't there an old Indian belief that a white god will come from the East to liberate the people?

Extraordinary, quite extraordinary. When you get back to Guatemala you must go on with it.'

'I am doing it now. In my room,' she said. 'You are my inspiration. I've been working every night since I saw you.'

'Shall I post this copy to your hotel in Berlin?' he said.

'No, give it to me when we meet there.'

'Berlin!' the editor exclaimed. Without thinking, without realizing what he was saying, the editor said: 'But I'm *not* going to Berlin. I'm going back to London at once.'

'When?' said the human voice. 'Could I come and talk to you now.'

'I'm afraid not. I'm leaving in half an hour,' said the editor. Only when he put the telephone receiver back did the editor realize that he was sweating and that he had told a lie. He had lost his head. Worse, in Berlin, if she were there, he would have to invent another lie.

It *was* worse than that. When he got to Berlin she was *not* there. It was perverse of him – but he was alarmed. He was ashamed: the shadiness of the saint replaced the pagan on his handsome face; indeed, on the race question, after his lecture a man in the audience said he was evasive.

But in Hamburg, at the end of the week, her voice spoke up from the back of the hall:

'I would like to ask the great man who has filled all our hearts this evening, whether he does not think that the worst racists are the oppressors and deceivers of women?'

She delivered her blow and sat down, disappearing behind the shoulders of bulky German men.

The editor's clever smiles went; he jerked back his heroic head as if he had been shot; he balanced himself by touching the table with the tips of his fingers. He lowered his head and drank a glass of water, splashing it on his tie. He looked for help.

'My friends,' he wanted to say, 'that woman is following

me. She has followed me all over Scandinavia and Germany. I had to tell a lie to escape from her in Berlin. She is pursuing me. She is writing a poem. She is trying to force me to read it. She murdered her father – I mean her father murdered her mother. She is mad. Someone must get me out of this.'

But he pulled himself together and sank to that point of desperation to which the mere amateurs and hams of public-speaking sink:

'A good question,' he said. Two irreverent laughs came from the audience, probably from the American or English colony. He had made a fool of himself again. Floundering, he at last fell back on one of those drifting historical generalizations which so often rescued him. He heard his voice sailing into the eighteenth century, throwing in Rousseau, gliding on to Tom Paine and *The Rights of Man*.

'Is there a way out of the back of this hall?' he said to the Chairman afterwards. 'Could someone keep an eye on that woman? She is following me.'

They got him out by a back door.

At his hotel a poem was slipped under his door.

Suckled on Rousseau
Strong in the divine message of Nature
Clasp Guatemala in your arms.

Room 363 was written at the end. She was staying at the same hotel! He rang down to the desk, said he would receive no calls, and demanded to be put on the lowest floor, close to the main stairs and near the exit. Safe in his new room, he changed the time of his flight to Munich. There was a note for him at the desk.

'Miss Mendoza left this for you,' said the clerk, 'when she left for Munich this morning.'

Attached to the note was a poem.

Ravenous in the long night of the centuries
I waited for my Liberator
He shall not escape me

it began. His hand was shaking as he tore up the note and the poem and made for the door. The page boy came running after him with the receipt for his bill which he had left on the desk.

The editor was a well-known man. Reporters visited him. He was often recognized in hotels. People spoke his name aloud when they saw it on passenger lists. Cartoonists were apt to lengthen his neck when they drew him, for they had caught his habit of stretching it at parties or meetings, hoping to see and be seen.

But not on the flight to Munich. He kept his hat on and lowered his chin. He longed for anonymity. He had a sensation he had not had for years, not indeed since the pre-thaw years in Russia: that he was being followed, not simply by one person but by dozens. Who were all these passengers on the plane? Had those two men in raincoats been at his hotel?

He made for the first car he saw at the airport. At the hotel he went to the desk:

'Mr and Mrs Macaulay Drood,' the clerk said. 'Yes. 415. Your wife has arrived.'

'My wife!' In any small group, the actor woke up in him. He turned from the clerk to a stranger standing at the desk beside him and gave a yelp of hilarity. 'But I am not married.' The stranger drew away. The editor turned to a couple also standing there. 'But I am saying I am not married,' he laughed. He turned about to see if he could gather more listeners.

'This is ludicrous,' he said. No one was interested and loudly to the clerk he said:

'Let me see the register. There is no Mrs Drood.'

The clerk put on an embarrassed but worldly look, to soothe any concern about the respectability of the hotel in the people who were waiting. But there, on the card, in her writing, were the words:

'Mr and Mrs M. Drood – London.'

The editor turned dramatically to the group.

'A forgery!' he cried. He laughed, inviting all to join the comedy. 'A woman travelling under my name.'

The clerk and the strangers turned away. In travel one can rely on there being one mad Englishman everywhere.

The editor's face darkened when he saw he had exhausted human interest.

'415. Baggage,' called the clerk.

A young porter came up quick as a lizard, and picked up the editor's bag.

'Wait. Wait,' said the editor. Before a young man so smoothly uniformed, he had the sudden sensation of standing there with most of his clothes off.

When you arrived at the Day of Judgement there would be some worldly youth, humming a tune you didn't know the name of, carrying not only your sins but your virtues indifferently in a couple of bags, and gleaming with concealed knowledge.

'I have to telephone,' the editor said.

'Over there,' said the young man and put the bags down. The editor did not walk to the telephone cabin, but to the main door of the hotel. He considered the freedom of the street. The sensible thing to do was to leave the hotel at once, but he saw that the woman would be at his lecture that night. He would have to settle the matter once and for all now. So he turned back to the telephone cabin. It stood there empty, like a trap. He walked past it. He hated the glazed, whorish, hypocritically impersonal look of telephone cabins. They were always unpleasantly warmed by random emotions left behind in them. He turned back; the thing was still empty. 'Surely,' he wanted to address the people coming and going in the foyer, 'someone wants to telephone?' It was wounding that not one person there was interested in his case. It was as if he had written an article that no one had read. Even the porter had gone. His two bags rested against the desk. He and they had ceased to be news.

He began to walk up and down quickly, but this stirred no one. He stopped in every observable position, not quite ignored now because his handsome hair always made people turn.

The editor silently addressed them. 'You've entirely missed the point of my position. Everyone knows who has read what I have written, that I am opposed to the whole idea of marriage on principle. That is what makes this woman's behaviour so ridiculous. To think of getting *married* in a world which is in one of the most ghastly phases of its history, is puerile.'

He gave a short sarcastic laugh. The audience was indifferent.

The editor went to the telephone box and leaving the door open for all to hear, he rang her room.

'Macaulay Drood,' he said brusquely. 'It is important that I should see you at once, privately, in your room.'

He heard her breathing. The way the human race thought it was enough if they breathed. Ask an important question and what happens? Breath. Then he heard the small voice: it made a splashing confusing sound.

'Oh,' it said. And more breath. 'Yes.'

The two words were the top of a wave that is about to topple and come thumping over on to the sand and then draws back with a long, insidious hiss.

'Please,' she added.

And the word was the long thirsty hiss.

The editor was surprised that his brusque manner was so wistfully treated. 'Good heavens,' he thought, 'she *is* in that room.' And because she was invisible, and because of the distance of the wire between them, he felt she was pouring down it, head first, mouth open, swamping him. When he put the telephone down, he scratched his ear; a piece of her seemed to be coiled there. The editor's ear had heard passion. And passion at its dramatic climax.

He had often heard of passion. He had often been told of it. He had often read about it. He had seen it in opera. He had friends – who usually came to him for advice – who were entangled in it. He had never felt it and he did not feel it now; but when he walked from the telephone cabin to the lift, he saw his role had changed. The woman was not a mere nuisance – she was something like Tosca. The pagan became doggish, the saint furtive as he entered the lift.

'Ah,' the editor burst out aloud to the liftman, 'les femmes.' The German did not understand French.

The editor got out of the lift and, passing one watchful white door after another, came to 415. He knocked twice: when there was no answer, he opened the door.

He seemed to blunder into an invisible wall of spice and scent and stepped back thinking he had made a mistake. A long-legged rag doll with big blue eyes looked at him from the bed, a half-unpacked suitcase was on the floor with curious clothes hanging out of it. A woman's shoes were tipped out on the sofa.

And there, standing by a small desk where she had been writing, was Miss Mendoza. Or rather the bottle green dress, the box-like figure were Miss Mendoza; the head was not. Her hair was no longer black; it was golden. The idol's had been chopped off and was replaced by a woman's. There was no expression on the face, until the shock on the editor's face sent shock to hers, then a searching look of horror seized her, and then of being caught in an outrage. Then she lowered her head, suddenly cowed and frightened. She quickly grabbed a stocking she had left on the bed and held it behind her back.

'You are angry with me,' she said, holding her head down like an obstinate child.

'You are in *my* room. You have no right to be here. I am very angry with you. What do you mean by registering in my name – apart from anything else it is illegal. You know that, don't you? I must ask you to go or I shall have to take steps ...'

Her head was still lowered. Perhaps he ought not to have said the last sentence. The blonde hair made her look pathetic.

'Why did you do this?'

'Because you would not see me,' she said. 'You have been cruel to me.'

'But don't you realize, Miss Mendoza, what you are doing? I hardly know you. You have followed me all over Europe, you have badgered me. You take my room. You pretend to be my wife ...'

'Do you hate me?' she muttered.

Damn, thought the editor, I ought to have changed my hotel at once.

'I know nothing about you,' he said.

'Don't you want to know about me? What I am like? I know everything about you,' she said, raising her head.

The editor was confused by the rebuke. His fit of acting passed. He looked at his watch.

'A reporter is coming to see me in half an hour,' he said.

'I shall not be in the way,' she said. 'I will go out.'

'*You* will go out!' said the editor. Then, he understood where he was going wrong. He had – perhaps being abroad, addressing meetings, speaking to audiences with only one mass face had done this – forgotten how he dealt with difficult people.

He pushed the shoes to one end of the sofa to find himself a place. One shoe fell to the floor but after all it was his room and he had a right to sit in it.

'Miss Mendoza, you are ill,' he said.

She looked down quickly at the carpet.

'I am not,' she said.

'You are ill and, I think, very unhappy.'

He put on his wise voice.

'No,' she said in a low voice. 'Happy. You are talking to me.'

'You are a very intelligent woman,' he said. 'And you will understand what I am going to say. Gifted people like yourself are very vulnerable. You live in the imagination and that exposes one. I know that.'

'Yes,' she said. 'You see all the injustices of the world. You bleed from them.'

'I? Yes,' said the editor with his saint's smile. But he recovered from the flattery. 'I am saying something else. Your imagination is part of your gift as a poet, but in real life it has deluded you.'

'It hasn't done that. I see you as you are.'

'Please sit down,' said the editor. He could not bear her standing over him. 'Close the window; there is too much noise.'

She obeyed. The editor was alarmed to see the zip of her green dress was half undone and he could see the top of some garment with ominous lace on it. He could not bear untidy women. He saw his case was urgent. He made a greater effort to be kind.

'It was very nice of you to come to my lectures. I hope you found them interesting. I think they went down all right – good questions. One never knows, of course. One arrives in a strange place and one sees a room, I mean a hall, full of people one doesn't know – and you won't believe it, perhaps, because I've done it scores of times – but one likes to see one face that one recognizes. One feels lost, at first . . .'

She looked hopefully.

This was untrue. The editor never felt lost. Once on his feet, he had the sensation that he was talking to the human race. He suffered with it. It was the general human suffering that had ravaged his face.

'But, you know,' he said sternly. 'Our feelings deceive us. Especially at certain times of life. I was worried about you. I saw something was wrong. These things happen very suddenly. God knows why – you see someone whom you admire, perhaps, and it seems to happen to women more than men – you project some forgotten love on them. You think you love them, but it is really some forgotten image. In your case, I would say, probably some image of your father whom you thought of all these years, since you hated what he did when you were a child – you told me the story. And so, as people say, one becomes obsessed or infatuated. I don't like the word. What we mean is that one is not in love with a real man or woman but a vision sent out by oneself. One can think of many examples . . .'

The editor was sweating. He wished he hadn't asked her to close the window. He knew his mind was drifting towards historic instances. He wondered if he would tell her the story of Mrs Carlyle, the wife of the historian, who had gone to hear the famous Father Matthew speak to a temperance meeting and how, hysterical and exalted, she had rushed to the platform to kiss his boots. There were other instances. For the moment he couldn't remember them. He decided on Mrs Carlyle. It was a mistake.

'Who is Mrs Carlyle?' said Miss Mendoza suspiciously. 'I would never kiss any man's feet.'

'Boots,' said the editor. 'It was on a public platform.'

'Or boots,' said Miss Mendoza and burst out. 'Why are you torturing me? You are saying I am mad.'

The editor was surprised by the turn of the conversation. It had seemed to be going well.

'Of course you're not mad,' he said. 'A mad woman could not have written that great poem. I am just saying that I value your feeling but you must understand I unfortunately do not love you. But you *are* ill. You have exhausted yourself.'

Miss Mendoza's yellowish eyes became brilliant as she listened to him.

'So,' she said grandly, 'I am a mere nuisance.'

She got up from her chair and he saw she was trembling.

'If that is so, why don't you leave this room at once,' she said.

'But,' said the editor with a laugh, 'if I may mention it, it is mine.'

'I signed the register,' said Miss Mendoza.

'Well,' said the editor smiling, 'that is not the point, is it?'

The boredom, the sense of the sheer waste of time (when one thought of the massacres, the bombings, the imprisonments in the world), in personal questions, overcame him. It amazed him how many times, at some awful crisis – the Cuban, for example – how many people left their husbands, wives or lovers, in a general post: the extraordinary, irresponsible persistence of outbreaks of love. A kind of guerrilla war in another context. Here he was in the midst of it. What could he do? He looked around the room for help. The noise of traffic outside in the street, the dim sight of people moving in office windows opposite, an advertisement for beer, were no help. Humanity had deserted him. The nearest thing to the human – now it took his eye – was the doll on the bed, an absurd marionette from the cabaret, the raffle or the nursery. It had a mop of red hair, silly red cheeks and popping blue eyes with long cotton lashes to them. It wore a short skirt and had long inane legs in check stockings. How childish women were. Of course (it now occurred to him) Miss Mendoza was as childish as her voice. The editor said playfully:

'I see you have a little friend. Very pretty. Does she come from Guatemala?' And frivolously, because he disliked the thing, he took a step or two towards it. Miss Mendoza pushed past him at once and grabbed it.

'Don't touch it,' she said with tiny fierceness.

She picked up the doll and hugging it with fear, she looked for somewhere to put it out of his reach. She went to the door, then changed her mind and rushed to the window with it. She opened the window and as the curtains blew in she looked as if one desperate idea had occurred to her – to throw it and herself out of the window. She turned to fight him off. He was too bewildered to move and when she saw that he stood still her frightened face changed. Suddenly she threw the doll on the floor and half falling on to a chair near to it, her shoulders rounded, she covered her face with her hands and sobbed, shaking her head from side to side. Tears crawled through her fingers down the backs of her hands. Then she took her hands away and soft and shapeless she rushed to the editor and clawed his coat.

'Go away. Go away,' she cried. 'Forgive me. Forgive. I'm sorry.' She began to laugh and cry at once. 'As you said – ill. Oh, please forgive. I don't understand why I did this. For a week I haven't eaten anything. I must have been out of my mind to do this to you. Why? I can't think. You've been so kind. You could have been cruel. You were right. You had the courage to tell me the truth. I feel so ashamed, so ashamed. What can I do?'

She was holding to his jacket. Her tears were on his hands. She was pleading. She looked up.

'I've been such a fool.'

'Come and sit here,' said the editor, trying to move her to the sofa. 'You are not a fool. You have done nothing. There is nothing to be ashamed of.'

'I can't bear it.'

'Come and sit here,' he said putting his arm on her shoulder. 'I was very proud when I read your poem. Look,' he said, 'you are a very gifted and attractive woman.'

He was surprised that such a heavy woman was not like iron to the touch, but light and soft. He could feel her skin hot through her dress. Her breath was hot. Agony was hot. Grief was hot. Above all her clothes were hot: it was perhaps because of the heat of her clothes that for the first time for years he had the sensation of holding a human being. He had never felt this when, on a few occasions, he had held a woman naked in her bed. He did something then that was incredible to himself when he did it: he gently kissed the top of her head, on the blonde hair he did not like. It was like kissing a heated mat and it smelled of burning.

At his kiss, she clawed no longer and her tears stopped. She moved away from him in awe.

'Thank you,' she said gravely and he found himself being studied, even memorized, as she had done when she had first come to his office. The look of the idol was set on her again. Then she uttered a revelation:

'You do not love anyone but yourself.'

And worse, she smiled. He had thought, with dread, that she was waiting to be kissed again, but now he couldn't bear what she said. It was a loss.

'We must meet,' he said recklessly. 'We *shall* meet at the lecture tonight.'

The shadow of her future passed over her face.

'Oh no,' she said. She was free. She was warning him not to hope to exploit her pain.

'This afternoon?' he said trying to catch her hand but she drew it away. And then, to his bewilderment she was dodging round him. She was packing. She began stuffing her few clothes into her suitcase. She went to the bathroom and while she was there the porter came in with his two bags.

'Wait,' said the editor.

She came out of the bathroom looking very pale and put the remaining things in her bag.

'I asked him to wait,' the editor said.

The kiss, the golden hair, the heat of her head seemed to be flying round in the editor's head.

'I don't want you to leave like this,' the editor said.

'I heard what you said to the man,' she said hurriedly shutting the case. 'Good-bye. And thank you. You have saved me from something dreadful.'

The editor could not move when he saw her go. He could not believe she had gone. He could feel the stir of her scent in the air; and he sat down exhausted but arguing with his conscience. Why had she said that about loving only himself? What else could he have done? He wished there were people there to whom he could explain, whom he could ask. He was feeling loneliness for one of the few times in his life. He went to the window to look down at the crowd and looking back to the bed he was astounded by a thought:

'I have never had an adventure in my life.'

And with that he left the room and went down to the desk. Was she still in the hotel?

'No,' said the desk clerk. 'Mrs Drood went off in a taxi.'

'I'm asking for Miss Mendoza.'

'No one of that name.'

'Extraordinary,' lied the editor. 'She was to meet me here.'

'Perhaps she is at the Hofgarten; it's the same management.'

For the next hour he was in that disastrous, mocking, whorish calm, trying all the hotels. He got a cab to the station; he tried the airlines and then, in the afternoon, went out to the airport. He knew it was hopeless. 'I must be mad,' he thought. He looked at every fair-haired woman he could see: the city was full of them it seemed to him. As the noisy city afternoon moved by he gave up. He liked to talk about himself but here was a day he could never describe to anyone. He could not bear to return to his room but sat in the lounge trying to read a paper, wrangling with himself and looking up at every woman who passed. He could not eat or even drink and when he went out to his lecture, he walked all the way to the hall on the chance of seeing her. He had the fancy once or twice, which he laughed at bitterly, that she had just passed and had left two or three of her foot prints on the pavement. The maddening thing was that she was exactly the kind of woman he could not bear – squat, ugly; how awful she must look without clothes on. He tried to exorcise her by obscene images. They vanished and some transformed, indefinable vision of her came back. He began to see her tall and dark; or young and fair; her eyes changing colour; voluptuously rounded, athletically slim. As he sat on the lecture platform, listening to the introduction, he made faces that astonished people by a mechanical display of eagerness followed by scorn, as his gaze went systematically from row to row, looking for her. He got up to speak – he knew it would be the best lecture he had ever given. It was. Urging, appealing, agonizing, eloquent: it was an appeal to her to come back.

And then, after a lot of discussion, which he hardly heard, he returned to the hotel. He had now to face the mockery of the room. He let himself in and it did mock. The maid had turned the bed back and on it lay the doll, its legs tidied, its big ridiculous eyes staring at him. They seemed to him to blink. She had forgotten it. She had left her childhood behind.

Ruth Fainlight

Soir de Fête

1 *The Pearls*

It was almost dark. Through open windows covered by venetian blinds, lights from the block of apartments opposite and noise from the cafe three floors below emphasized the surrounding activity. A burst of laughter sounded as loud as if in the same room. They looked at each other, startled; then Charles laughed as if he too had heard the joke.

While Betty fastened her gold-linked belt and bracelets and Ann crouched by the bedside to adjust a sandal, he stood squarely in front of the long mirror, tanned face thrust upwards to facilitate the setting of shirt collar beneath his jacket, then pivoted slowly to study his posture, viewing the reflection with sad, dark eyes. Although nearly fifty, his body was that of an athletic young man, its care and study being his most time-absorbing interest. It was only when he tried to talk seriously that his face lost its confident expression and dissolved into uncertainty.

'Let's have a drink before we go,' Betty suggested. 'Wouldn't you like a drink?' She pulled back her head to look searchingly into Ann's eyes. Under the direct glare of the ceiling light all lines and hollows were accentuated, changing an attractive blonde of forty-five into an old woman. After a few moments she sensed this unfortunate contrast to the dark girl half her age, and hid her face altogether by kissing Ann's shoulder.

Ann had met Betty and Charles a week ago at a cafe on the sea-front. As the reasons for this rapidly developed friendship seemed to be connected with loneliness and weakness she preferred not to analyse them. After saving enough money for the trip, she had come to Europe filled with immense and nebulous desires, ambitions and excitement. Perhaps she would write a novel, or be discovered by a film director. Charles and Betty represented all she had rejected, everything that made her uneasy and angry and awkward, and had led her to cut herself off from her family until they did not even know where she was. Yet she was glad to have met them and to go out with them, to talk about America and postpone from day to day the realization of how lost she felt on this continent where no one knew of her existence. Being with Charles and Betty was like a continuation of the irresponsible life on the boat coming over, and when they suggested she share the apartment they had just taken, she agreed. Lurking at the back of her mind were ideas about the relative positions of rich retired shopkeepers looking for a good time, and young artists who might be supported by them. She had moved in that morning, the Quinze Août.

Charles poured the drinks. But after 'Good Health', there was nothing to say. They stood silently at one side of the scented bedroom near the large mirror in which they were pinkly reflected, and the flashes of light as they tilted the wine glasses were repeated from their moving eyes furtively glancing at one another, from the crumpled shimmer of Betty's nightdress on the arm of a padded chair by the window, and the highlighted folds of her dresses hanging in the open wardrobe. The drink renewed their feelings of friendship, and Charles sighed, licked his lips, and said, 'Ah, that was good.' He put his glass down with a clink on the glass top of the dressing table, and reaching out to touch Ann, demanded, 'Well, are you enjoying yourself?'

'Of course she is. What a question!' Betty cut in, glaring at her husband. 'Of course you're enjoying yourself, aren't you, darling?' she insisted. 'And how nice you look. Don't you think Ann looks nice, Charles? But I think she needs something around her neck, don't you?' She spoke as if this were his cue.

'Do you really think so? I thought I looked fine.'

'Oh no,' Betty told her, sitting down on the edge of the bed. 'That blouse is much too plain. What you need is some sort of necklace.'

Twisting around to view the effect of the pale blouse and silk suit borrowed from Betty, Ann sounded dubious. 'Really?'

'Go on,' Betty murmured. Charles fumbled in his pocket, then withdrew a two-stranded pearl necklace which he held up, slung between outraised hands, like a magician at the successful climax of a trick. But Ann did not even trouble to take it, and after glancing over her shoulder, carelessly said, 'Oh no, thank you, that wouldn't do.' She picked up a tube of lipstick and leaned forward to peer in the glass, and did not notice when he walked silently out of the room.

Before Betty could speak he was back. After scrutinizing the bewildered face of her husband, she kept her head lowered and appeared to be studying her fingernails.

Noise from the street became louder and more hilarious as people began to crowd down to the promenade for the fête. Disturbed air eddied through the slats of the blind, bringing snatches of speech and laughter. With a stubborn expression, Charles pulled the necklace out of his pocket again. Betty eyed him disapprovingly. Seeing he would receive no help from her, he sat down, and said weakly, 'Look Ann. Come here. Don't you think this is pretty?'

She was opening one of Betty's bottles of perfume, and

turned sharply at her name, shocked to see how embarrassed he looked, then escaped back into the depths of the mirror. Her reflected face was stiff with an indignation she could hardly understand. Charles made a pretence of sauntering out of the room, and in the corridor began whistling loudly.

Betty watched Ann until she saw that her flush had faded, then slowly said, 'I really am surprised at you. I didn't know you were so silly.'

'What do you mean?' Her colour mounted again.

'Don't you know?' Betty continued, maddeningly placid. 'If a man wants to give you a present you should accept it. You've only made Charles feel a fool. You certainly should have taken the necklace when he offered it to you. He was very hurt.'

In a confusion of embarrassment, anger, and dislike, Ann countered, 'But I didn't know he was offering it to me as a gift. I thought he was just suggesting I wear it now – that it was yours – or something –'

'And why should he offer to lend it to you if it was mine?' Betty scornfully asked. 'You were just stupid. Now go to Charles and say you've changed your mind. And do it nicely,' she counselled. 'I thought you knew already what bad policy it was to refuse a gift.'

'I can't go in and ask him!'

'Don't be silly,' Betty insisted. 'It's a good necklace and you'll be very happy to have it one day. You need some pretty things. And you'll make Charles happy, too. I should know him by now, we've been married for over twenty years. Now go on, do as I tell you,' she said, taking Ann by the arm and pushing her towards the door. 'Go on.'

In the corridor Ann stopped, looked for support from her reflection in the gilt-framed mirror on the wall, and tried to imagine that reflection with the addition of the necklace in only a few minutes more. But those minutes seemed so difficult to accept that she was tempted to run down the stairs away from them both. Then a door opened, and she turned to find Betty silently on guard. Resigning herself, she said loudly into the air, 'I really think those pearls would look nice –' and saw Betty's nod of approval, a nod that quickly became a commanding glare of interrogation when she did not move. She tapped Charles's door, and at the same moment Betty slipped back into her room.

'Why don't you come in?' he asked, taking her hand. 'Come on in.' On his desk the necklace gleamed in the dim light from the bed lamp.

'You know, I think I do need something to wear around my neck after all,' she blurted out.

'Oh yes, I agree with you. I knew you'd like this necklace.' He sounded relieved. 'Let me put it on for you and we'll see how it looks.'

She bent her head forward solemnly, and he lifted her collar to fasten the clasp. Through the thin cloth of the blouse she could feel the beads' weight and coldness.

'Betty!' Charles called. 'Betty, come in here.' He put an arm around Ann's shoulders, and turned with her to face the door. 'Doesn't she look fine?' he said gaily as Betty entered, already smiling.

'She certainly does, and you both look much happier. Very pretty.' Kissing Ann, she whispered, 'There, isn't that better?' then asked aloud, 'Now, have you thanked him?'

'Of course,' Charles said, but she insisted, 'No, you must kiss him.'

Ann touched his cheek with her lips and mumbled, 'Thank you,' as if betraying her closest friend.

'Come on,' Betty said briskly. 'We'd better get going.'

In the hall Charles stopped them at the mirror. 'Doesn't she look pretty?'

'Make sure you lock the door,' Betty called as she rang for the elevator. The safety doors opened and they stepped into the brightly lit cage and descended to the carnival.

2 *The Confetti*

All streets leading to the promenade were crowded, and even before reaching the barrier they were slowed down. Near the pay box, men had established themselves with stocks of confetti. When Charles saw them he broke away, returning in a moment with three bags of the largest size. He looked about gleefully, as if anticipating all the confetti he was going to throw that night; then he bought their tickets, and they passed through the barrier onto the seafront, where rows of people already waited along the pavement. In the movement and glitter and noise of the hot night it was impossible to believe that the cool, indifferent sea lay only yards away.

Elated and restless, they prowled in the narrow pathway left between spectators and the low walls of hotels, laughing shrilly at every remark and tossing confetti at each other, while the procession passed and they hardly saw it. Only sometimes where the line of watchers thinned could they catch sight of a float bearing a group of girls in one sort of costume or other; now flowers, now pierrots, now slaves in an eastern market with their arms held by the wrist to a pole, looking as uncomfortable as if they really were slaves, but smiling down at the crowd. Charles pranced ahead with three new bags of confetti pushed under one arm, hurling it into the face of anyone who caught his eye.

'Let me have some more confetti, Charles. Look, mine is

finished.' Betty ran up to him, panting with laughter. 'Come on, let me have some more.'

Saying nothing, in a sudden movement he emptied a bag of it over her head. Confetti streamed onto hair, face, and the front of her dress.

'You bastard!' she shouted, pushing him with one hand, spitting away the pieces of paper stuck to her lips as if she wanted them to hit his face. A group of boys paused to watch, but Charles bombarded them until they moved on. He put his arm around her roughly and said, 'Here, keep quiet, here's another bag,' then hurried ahead.

Betty waited, sulkily brushing her clothes. 'Look what that pig has done,' she complained, picking at the clinging confetti. 'He threw the stuff all over me. Let's give him the same.' Although not sure whether she wanted to become involved in Betty's revenge, Ann agreed, and they joined hands and forced a slow way through the crowd which, now the procession was over, milled against them.

In this way they reached the far end of the promenade. They found Charles here, and one on each side, holding his arms to keep him captive, retreated into the shallow curve of a gateway. 'So we've got you at last!' Betty said, no longer angry, merely sprinkling a few discs of confetti over his head as a token of triumph. But Ann threw her handful directly into his face, with a surge of hatred for his continual laughter.

Shaking his head, he blindly threw some back. She zigzagged around groups of people, and for a few minutes he could not catch her. But she was trapped by the high wall of a villa. Pressing her against it with his strong body, he systematically poured confetti into her hair, smeared it into her face, and did not stop until the bag was empty. Several people passing looked interested or censorious, but no one interfered until Betty arrived.

'Leave her alone now,' she said indignantly. Charles stared as if coming out of a dream, and abruptly stopped laughing. When Ann had spat the last of the dry, sour powderiness from her mouth he had disappeared. 'He really doesn't know when to stop,' Betty said. 'He gets too cruel. Are you all right, darling?'

Ann stared forlornly at the people passing by. She hugged Betty's arm as they strolled on. But after a few minutes their arms dropped apart, and they were laughing as loudly as the rest. A group of three young men began to follow them, edging around with fixed grins and speaking the hard, ugly French used by Germans. Their white faces had a cold and greasy shine, their clothes were dark, and one of them wore an open leather wind-jammer. Betty laughed, as if there could be nothing more amusing than this little procession following them so determinedly. Her tanned face and golden jewellery caught the direct light of a decorated street lamp, and, dishevelled hair scattered with little coloured discs of confetti, confetti lodged in the lattice-worked bodice of her dress like snow upon a statue, she seemed a barbaric personification of the carnival. The young man in the leather jacket came closer, as if enthralled. Delighted by his attentions, Betty swaggered along, poking fun at him in every language of which she could muster a few words.

They were nearing the central part of the promenade, and with each step became more enclosed in the crowd that thickened around and behind them. A few yards away Ann saw Charles, and pushed forward until they were abreast. When she touched him he stared back with blank, unrecognizing eyes for a moment before stopping. Under one arm he held a half-empty bag of confetti, but already he was bored.

At that moment the German grasped Betty's arm. She looked about, trying to find Charles or Ann, then hurried over with an expression of relief.

'He was getting on my nerves,' she said breathlessly. 'He's been pestering me all the way.'

For a moment they stood on a raised curb, then tried to re-enter the crowd. But now each person was so tightly jammed against the next that they could not do so. Speech and laughter came from the hotel terrace behind, but there was little noise from this group, whose efforts to churn their way forward only packed them tighter. Ann suddenly felt frightened, and at the same moment the first general wave of uneasiness manifested itself. She realized what a bad position they were in, caught between the fence and the crowd. 'We must move,' she said, and pushed a few feet further on.

'Are you O.K.?' Charles asked, pulling her around. She did not seem to hear him, and he could almost share the claustrophobic visions in her dilated eyes. He kept hold of her arm, wondering how they could get out. 'We'd better stay put until they start moving again,' he said. 'All right?'

From the centre of the crowd a woman screamed. An answering cry burst so startlingly from Ann's throat that for a moment it succeeded in breaking her hysteria. But these two shrill outcries had jangled everyone's nerves.

Behind the picket fence was a hedge of the same height, and behind that, the stone wall of a hotel terrace. The thin wooden fence bent backwards on each side of them as the pressure grew. Turning to grasp the top of one of the pickets before she lost her balance, two of Ann's fingers were trapped against the stones. She screamed again; Charles jumped onto the top of the wall, and dragged her over the sagging fence and hedge up to him. Then he reached for Betty, whose full-skirted petticoat caught and ripped loudly, leaving a long strip of lace fluttering like the bullet-torn flag at an abandoned barricade.

They had entered an entirely different world, the terrace of a luxurious hotel, where well-dressed and composed holiday-makers turned to look with surprise at these creatures who had erupted upon them. As they sat down at an empty table, Ann laughed tremulously and said, 'Imagine acting like that!'

'You must try to keep calm,' Betty admonished. 'Because otherwise you'll get hurt. But of course you will. It's all right, honey, nothing wrong with getting a little scared,' she finished more comfortingly. 'You're all right now, aren't you?'

Ann did not want to admit how humiliated she felt, but only to prove that she was not as stupid or helpless as they must think her.

'Sure, she's all right,' Charles said indifferently. 'Let's have a drink.' But on the crowded terrace he found it difficult to catch the waiter's eye. After ten minutes of useless gesticulating and of calls that seemed to be absorbed into the air before reaching anyone, he pulled himself out of his chair. 'Let's get out of here,' he muttered, and brusquely led them from the hotel into a cool and quiet side street.

At the first bar they stopped for a drink. Feeling sick, Ann left for a moment. Coming back from the cloakroom she saw them talking earnestly, and before the grating sound of her pulled-back chair made them aware of her presence, heard Betty say, 'Yes, the beach would be a good place.'

'We were just talking about the best place to see the fireworks,' she explained. 'There's still a big crowd on the promenade. How about going down to the beach? It'll be nice and quiet there, and we'll have a good view.'

'That sounds fine,' Ann agreed inattentively. Bending to adjust a buckle, she saw the little bright circles of confetti which had slipped through her toes during the evening, pressed into the sandal soles and being carried away by her from the fête.

Charles gulped down his drink and ordered another. He drank so rarely, following the regime he hoped would keep him young and potent forever, that two glasses of brandy and the wine before leaving the apartment were enough to make him drunk. He began to laugh. 'You're having a good time, aren't you, honey?' he asked Ann. 'You like Betty and me, don't you? We'll give you a good time.'

'Come on,' Betty interrupted. 'We'll miss the fireworks if we don't get down to the beach.'

3 *The Stones*

Through dim, confusing beams of light from the promenade, the moon, and the sea, they stumbled over smooth oval-shaped stones.

'Haven't we come too far?' Ann asked, but Betty answered reassuringly that further along they would have an even better view. Leading the way across the sloping expanse of the shore, at last she stopped by the sea-wall and sat down in its shadow. They leaned back, Ann uncomfortable between them, feeling the heat from their bodies and smelling the drink on their breaths. Then she was distracted by a sound like a piece of silk being violently ripped, and forgot them. The first firework had gone up.

A bursting rocket lit Charles's face. 'I bought this bottle at the bar,' he said, putting an arm around her. 'Have a drink.'

Still dominated by the idea that she must prove herself a good sport, Ann took a sip of brandy.

'Don't hog it,' Betty said, sliding a hand across her wrist. 'Give me a drop, honey.'

'Come on, loosen up, sweetheart,' Charles slurred as the

bottle went round again. 'Aren't you having a good time?'

'Sure she's having a good time,' Betty said.

Plumes of light drifted across the black sky and paled the sea a moment as they fell.

'Why don't you make yourself comfortable? Come on, there's nothing to be afraid of,' Charles coaxed, dragging Ann's head against his shoulder and clumsily kissing her.

'Why don't you kiss him, Ann? He's nice. Go on, kiss him! Don't be shy, I won't mind.'

On the empty beach she had a recurrence of the choking fear that had mastered her in the press of the crowd, and the same impulse which had almost made her run out of the apartment. Pushed against the stony wall and the stones of the beach, she tried to slide away, but the treacherous pebbles shifted under her and it seemed as if she were only digging herself deeper. Fireworks lifted against the night and rained down into the sea, alternately darkening and revealing their faces.

'Hey, what's the matter?' Charles asked irritably when he felt her shiver. 'What're you so nervous about? Don't you want a bit of fun?' He emphasized his words by pressing her down onto the stones.

'Leave me alone,' she muttered, trying to evade him.

'Don't be a baby,' Betty wheedled. 'We only want to enjoy ourselves and want you to enjoy yourself, too. There's no harm in it.'

'Sure,' Charles said. 'We can have a lot of fun if you like. It'll be so nice. When we first saw you we thought how nice you'd be.'

'You just be a good girl and see how much you like it,' Betty added. 'You won't be sorry if you do.'

'I don't want to,' Ann pleaded.

'Listen to her!' Charles proclaimed to the whole night. 'I thought she was so broad-minded!'

Betty tried to soothe him. Roused by his wife's kisses, Charles now directed his attentions to Ann. With the hopelessness of her position emphasized by the regular, indifferent rise and fall of the elaborate set pieces heralding the finale, she called out in despair.

Husband and wife turned to each other, unconsciously relaxing their hold. The moment she became aware of this, Ann tried to stand up. Before considering what he was doing, Charles crashed her down with a blow from his elbow.

'For God's sake, keep quiet!' Betty commanded. But the hysteria aroused by the fête now burst out in full force, and her cries rang against the stone wall and down the beach. The roar from the crowds almost drowned them, but Betty, maddened by the noise and its possible danger, pressed her hand over Ann's mouth. She snatched it away in a moment, and exclaimed, 'The little bitch! She bit my hand!'

'I'll keep her quiet,' Charles said menacingly. 'Here, hold her legs.'

'Be careful of the suit,' Betty remarked irrelevantly. 'It's a good one.' She slid around to take his place.

'She's biting me too,' he said in drunken amazement. 'I'll stop her.' He covered her mouth again, then settled himself more comfortably and reached for the brandy bottle. 'She sure is wild,' he said, taking a swallow. 'But all the better. She should calm down in a few minutes and then we can talk some sense.'

'Don't press too hard,' Betty warned jokingly.

'Don't worry,' he assured her.

An enormous illumination filled the sky, and they both turned to look. As he swivelled his head Charles unthinkingly put all his weight on the hand over Ann's face. He did not notice her struggles, and it was some minutes until the last firework blossomed, dissolved, and faded, and left them in a darkness in which they could barely see. Bending towards Ann again, Charles remarked, 'She seems O.K. now.'

'Are you feeling better, sweetheart?' Betty asked, loosening her hold from the girl's legs, but there was no answer. 'Take your hand away,' she advised her husband. 'She probably can't talk.'

Betty crouched down to look. Blinded by the fireworks, she was not sure of what she saw. She began shaking Ann's shoulder. 'Ann, Ann,' she demanded urgently. 'Oh, my God, Charles!' she cried.

'What's the matter?' he asked peevishly. They stared at each other in the dim light, eyes glowing with fear. 'I couldn't have!' he said. When Betty lifted Ann's head it rolled loosely, then dropped back when she released it, the pearl necklace chinking against the stones.

The promenade and town were silent. The crowd was still dazed by the display, but even as they remained on the beach they could hear the shuffling of dispersal, and voices rising again. Scrambling to her feet, Betty tugged at Charles's hand. 'Come on, we've got to get away from here before someone comes. Let's go.'

He stared at the still figure on the stones. 'I told you it was crazy to bring her onto the beach. None of your ideas are ever any good.'

'Let's get away from here,' Betty hissed. She pulled at him until he stood upright, then hurried to the first set of wooden steps leading to the promenade. 'Come on, Charles,' she implored. She looked carefully about, but no one noticed them. They slipped into the stream of moving people, and lost themselves in the last gaieties of the fête.

Ruth Fainlight

The Expatriates

It was one of those grey Mediterranean afternoons, when the black, unchanging pines sough mournfully and autumnally even though it is already March, and thick clouds blowing across the sky threaten rain for days. Jeanette Coleman lay in bed. Terrible, that's how I feel, terrible, her brain throbbed sluggishly, and in obedience to its signals, her arm lifted to the cluttered bed table for the tube of Alka Seltzer and some water. The carafe was empty; the only available liquid a half-empty glass of stale rum she must have carried upstairs early that morning. Complaining aloud at this negligence, she rang. The single word, '*Agua*,' greeted the maid's appearance. '*Y cigarillos*,' the hoarse voice added. 'And be quick about it,' Jeanette muttered to the closing door, as the girl hurried to the kitchen to warn the others.

She picked up a mirror, looked at herself, then let it drop among the bedclothes. The afternoon light, filtered through the pine trees, cold and direct from the sea, added ten years to her thirty-four. But the reflection somehow stiffened her spirit, and she reached for the phone. 'Hello?' she slurred, slumping back onto the pillows when the connection was made. 'Hello, Joe? This is Jeanette. Sure. Listen, have you got something to eat? Good. Send over a cab in about half an hour, will you? Good. Thanks. So long.'

She hung up, and relapsed into a reverie in which how terrible the moulded plaster ceiling was and how terrible she felt had equal parts, until the maid returned.

'I want a bath,' she said. '*Bano, sabe?*' Nodding her head vigorously, the girl went to start it running. Jeanette took her Alka Seltzer, dragged herself out of bed, and in just under an hour, made-up, dressed, and having consumed a glass of rum and half-smoked several cigarettes, she was ready to present herself to the world: a small, slightly plump, well-dressed blonde with protuberant blue eyes and sullen mouth, and with enough money to be popular. She hurried downstairs and through the large dark hall to the waiting taxi, while the servants began to lay the table on which they would eat the meal they had been preparing for her all morning.

'Hello, Jeanette,' Joe called as she came through the door with her unsteady walk. 'Come and sit down.' He was a tall Englishman of forty, who made as much money by various dubious aspects of the tourist business as he did by his bar's high prices. 'What a night!' she said as greeting. 'Why the hell do we drink so much?' Without waiting for an answer, she took a cigarette from her handbag and leaned across to him. 'Light?'

'I'm hungry,' she continued. 'What's to eat?' Again not waiting for his reply, she looked down at her wrists and asked, 'Did you find a bracelet here this morning? Either I lost it, or one of the damned maids took it. Like this, look.' She raised one hand, over which a heavy gold bangle slipped. 'I just can't keep a thing here. Everything gets lost or stolen.' 'You should be more careful, Jeanette,' Joe said sententiously. 'You're too careless, the way you leave things lying around. You can't trust anyone here, I should know.' 'You're right about that,' she agreed petulantly. 'I was looking through Dick's things yesterday, and half his stuff is gone. Either the maids have taken it, or that damned male nurse – practicante, or whatever they call them. When I first heard that word I thought it meant a midwife.'

'How is Dick, anyway?' Joe asked, voice strained with the effort to seem concerned. 'He's still in that damned clinic, having shock treatment, and God knows what else done to him, and he can't understand a thing, or tell anyone what he wants. It makes me sick to think about it, you know Joe. I would never have brought him over to Europe with me if I'd known this would happen – but he seemed all right. He said he wanted to come.' Her voice became tremulous as it rose. 'Tell the waiter to bring a drink over, will you? Thanks. You know what it's like, Joe. That damned doctor comes over every day, and says, '*Muy bien*,' and I don't know what's happening. You know how wonderful Dick is, a real gentleman, hospitable –' She reached for the drink as the waiter approached, and gulped it down. The tortured look that had given her face expression for a moment left it, and her undistinguished features reasserted themselves. 'I just don't know what to do. I don't know whether to leave him in that clinic, or take him back to the States. What do you think?' The direct question disconcerted him; he wanted to avoid answering. 'The best thing is not to worry. He's being looked after, and it's better for you that he's not in the house. He's not able to drink in the clinic, anyway. He must be hell to live with when he's sick – oh, of course, he's a wonderful person, but even the best of husbands can be annoying at times, can't they?' He laughed and patted her hand. 'Now relax, and tell me what you want to eat.'

'Yes,' she answered, voice husky again as she smiled. 'You're right, I'll eat. Not much, though.' She looked impatiently around the room, and uttered a short, hard laugh. Dust under the tables and stains on the upholstery were visible near the unshuttered windows. 'You shouldn't let anyone in here until dark, you know, Joe. Or have the place cleaned up, anyway. I used to have a bar, back in the States. You're letting yourself go.' 'I don't know about that,' he laughed defensively. Who did she think she was? he thought. 'What about that bar idea we were talking about? The season'll be on us before we know, and it's about time to get something going.' He'd clean up – in that sense, at least, if he could persuade her to make him the manager.

'I hope it is a good idea. It'll give Dick something to do. He's always wanted to do something, but he never could. He's never done anything; never had to,' she mused bitterly. 'His mother and father were both dead before he was eighteen, so he was left with plenty of money. You know, sometimes he'll pretend he has worked. I remember once in a cab he started talking to the driver telling him how he'd driven one; and with a doctor once, because his father was a doctor and he knew the jargon. He'll always try to convince the man he's with that he's done the same job, as if he's ashamed.' 'The bar should make him happy, anyway,' Joe steered her back to the point. 'Will you be able to get it?' A waiter walked indolently past the table. 'Pepe,' he called, and turned to Jeanette. 'Some steak, omelette? All right, steak. Bring two steaks, will you, Pepe? Well, the most important thing is to get it fixed up. I'll be able to leave this place a lot, Pepe's a good barman, and he's more or less honest.'

But the details of this idea formulated during several evenings of drinking did not seem to interest Jeanette at that moment. She was still pushing pieces of the steak around her plate long after Joe had finished. With bent head and shoulders slightly bowed, eyebrows contracted and mouth drooping, she began to twist the various rings on her large hands. 'For God's sake, Joe! I can't eat a thing,' she cried. 'Don't you have anything in the place to drink?' She took a small ampoule from her handbag, shook a tablet from it, and held it carefully until the drink came.

It was eight o'clock when Jeanette arrived home. The taxi pulled up the steep hill and turned into the drive. A strong moist wind whirled her skirt as she walked up the shallow steps that led to the house. In the darkness it seemed to lean forward; the balconies looked insecure, the three tall storeys and the tower oppressed her with their simultaneous solidity and meaninglessness. Even though she normally liked big houses – everything big appealed to her – this house was somehow too big. But for Dick it had been too small, and he had screamed and cursed through the rooms, banging on the walls and throwing furniture at them as he raged against its confinement. It must be hell in that clinic, she thought, in that tiny room, with his feet hanging off a bed too short for him.

She walked through the hall into the living room, irritated that no one had heard her enter, and irritated even more, and startled for a moment, to see seated by the fire a figure which revealed itself to be the inanely grinning son of the cook. 'What the hell are you doing in here?' she demanded, and glared as he slunk out of the room. She turned on the radio, then sat down, avoiding the chair he had vacated. The fire needed more wood, but the basket was empty. The bell was on the opposite wall, and although crossing the room to ring it offered the possibility of action, her aimlessness was only aggravated by the need to do the smallest thing. Instead, she kicked at the half-burned logs until they collapsed into dully-glowing small chunks which threw off such heat that she was forced to push back her chair. The music from the radio stopped; she began walking from one end of the room to the other, looking at everything with jaded eyes, at the mirror-topped tables, the mottled walls, the ostentatious and unused piano, the bad paintings of the owner's children, the horrible wall lights; hating this expensive, ugly, and inconvenient house in which she felt trapped. She picked up her coat, hoping that in some bar something was happening that might distract her, when one of the doors quietly opened, and a man's voice blurring the words by a strong central European accent said, 'Why, Jeanette, I was just coming to see you. Are you going out?'

'Oh, Max! I was so damned bored! Go to the kitchen and tell them to bring some wood, will you? And get some drinks.' 'Of course, Jeanette,' he answered obediently, like a well-trained major-domo. He had met her in that capacity, being the reception clerk at the hotel she had stayed at before taking a house.

'Well, Jeanette,' he said, putting several bottles on the table, and sitting down in the same armchair the cook's son had used. 'The wood will be here in a moment. How are you feeling today? Would you like a drink?' He gave her a shrewd look that was at the same time naïve in its candid calculation. He was only twenty-four, though, and would soon learn to disguise that expression. Otherwise, his smooth, colourless face and thin, slightly twisted lips struck exactly the right balance between obsequiousness and arrogance. 'I told you how I felt – damned bored. Nothing's happened, I haven't even had a report about Dick. I went to Joe's bar this afternoon –' 'Have you heard about his wife?' Max interrupted, a cruel and pettish smile lighting his long eyes. 'No.' Jeanette leaned forward. 'What happened? She's a real bitch, that Nina.' 'Oh, nothing, really. She got drunk last night and burst into the bar, you know, where Joe was talking to some woman, and made a most terrible scene. It was an Englishwoman staying at the hotel. She came back and told us all about it. She had to,' he giggled appreciatively. 'Nina had scratched her face up.'

'I'm feeling hungry, aren't you, Max?' Jeanette asked. 'I haven't eaten a thing all day.' 'Haven't they cooked?' he said, indignant and pompous, as if discussing staff at the hotel. 'I'll go out and see what there is. What would you like?' 'Oh, there should be some meat. Some cold meat, or a sandwich, something like that.' He shook his head as he stood up; such lack of interest he could not understand. The telephone rang. His smooth, multi-lingual voice began a rapid conversation in Spanish. 'That was the clinic. They say that Dick is all right, but he still wants to come out.' 'Oh, God,' Jeanette moaned. 'Fix me a drink first, then we can talk about this. I just don't know what to do.' 'Listen, Jeanette,' he said, handing her a filled glass. 'Don't worry for the moment. You have enough to think about as it is.' He looked around the room as he spoke. To him, its style meant luxury, and he felt that the possibility of enjoying it would be hampered by the too-sudden return of Jeanette's husband. 'Just relax now, and I'll go and get something to eat. They haven't brought the wood yet, anyway. I'll really have to do something about those people.'

Like her other confidantes, Max had no interest in what became of Dick, but he knew he must listen. 'Shall I bring the sandwiches over, or will you come to the table?' 'Oh, over here,' she murmured vaguely. Giving her the plate, he sat down by the fire. A large studio portrait of Dick Coleman, showing the face of an effeminately good-looking man, stared at him from a side table. It had been taken seventeen years before, when Dick was twenty-three, and Max thought that even then he had looked completely insane. But to open the conversation he remarked, 'Dick was very handsome when that was taken.' She turned around in her chair, and mournfully scrutinized the photograph. 'Yes, that was when we were first supposed to get married,' she said. 'He'd just come back from Europe. He'd gone away after his mother and father killed themselves.

'I thought he was wonderful then. I was only seventeen, and he seemed terrifically sophisticated. And he was very handsome. Of course, he was depressed a lot of the time, but we all thought it was natural. Well, the night before the wedding, Dick came over to our place. I was in my room packing, I remember. I was very excited. He sat down and asked me, "Honey, are you happy?" Of course I was, I told him.' Jeanette leaned forward in the chair, her gaze so intent that Max, unaware she was looking through him, did not know what expression to adopt. 'And then,' she said, her eyes shifting their focus, staring now as if she were trying to impress something of the utmost importance on him, 'he took a gun out of his pocket and said, "I'm happy, too. I'm so happy that I don't think I'll ever be happier. And you're happier than you'll ever be, too. So I'm going to kill you, and kill myself. There's no point in living any more now."'

Max was so interested in her story that he did not even remember to keep his usual expression of sardonic contempt. 'What did you do?' 'I screamed,' she said dryly. 'My mother and father came running in and took Dick downstairs. Of course we didn't get married. He went away, and a month later I married someone else.' 'And Dick?' Max asked. He refilled their glasses. 'Oh, he got married, too. But that only lasted a few weeks, then his wife divorced him and he went into a clinic. My marriage broke up after about three years, then I went home and found him there, living with my parents, and they'd never even told me. Well, we did get married, and since then,' she said, her voice swinging bitterly out of reminiscence which, no matter how unhappy, was at least in the past, and forward to the unhappy present, 'he's been in and out of clinics, more or less as you've seen him. Oh,' she moaned. 'He's so nice sometimes – he seems perfectly all right, and we can have such a good time, and then he'll just go off. And now I don't know what to do.' They had come full circle, and Max's features returned to their public mould.

'You'll have to stop worrying, Jeanette,' he said. 'You'll drive yourself crazy, as well. There's nothing you can do now. You have the best doctors here looking after him. You mustn't worry so much.' He continued in this style for a time, then imperceptibly changed his tone. He built up the dying fire, brought the bottles nearer his chair, and turned on the radio. It was two o'clock in the morning, but he found some late-night dance music. He yawned surreptitiously. After a day of work at the hotel, these evenings were very exhausting. He knew that Jeanette would not want to go to bed for hours. Even then she would have to be coaxed, and, like a child, would rather fall asleep in front of the fire than admit the day was finished. And as long as she remained awake she expected him to entertain her. There was really only one method of getting her to bed. But he had convinced himself that his reason for allowing night after night to pass with no more than an occasional kiss was because a direct advance would ruin everything; and her acceptance of this situation made him even less confident. Drunk and tired, he sat on the padded arm of her chair and put a hand on her shoulder. 'Jeanette,' he murmured. 'You're so pretty.' Tentatively kissing her cheek, he was surprised and encouraged when she did not resist. When she turned her head to respond, though, he was almost frightened. She was kissing him; her arms were around his neck and he was almost sliding onto her lap. He tried to draw away to regain his balance. Jeanette misinterpreted this action. Standing up with alacrity, so that they were both on their feet at the same moment, she kissed him again and then said, 'Sure, let's go up to bed.' Slightly dazed, he followed her up the stairs.

Dick Coleman sat at the mirror-topped table in the living-room with a newspaper, a pot of coffee and plate of sandwiches, and his clean, stiff hands reflected in its silvery depths. It was about ten o'clock, and a clear morning. He had been home from the clinic five days. A male nurse had come also, but yesterday Dick had thrown him out.

The first day had been wonderful, only spoiled by the fact that Jeanette would not let him have anything to drink. But he had been too tired to be seriously annoyed, and by the next morning had already hidden the bottle he bribed a maid to buy. In the afternoon they went for a drive and only stopped at one bar, returning in time for the doctor's visit. Although Dick felt very tired, he was downstairs when Max arrived from the hotel after dinner. Relenting, Jeanette allowed him a nightcap, not aware he had been sipping furtively from his own store all day. That final drink almost sent him to sleep, but he had not been entirely insensible, and heard Max say, 'What shall we do now he's back?' Jeanette hushed him peremptorily, and bent over that carefully held deception of slumber. Apparently reassured, she nevertheless answered in a way that to Dick seemed evasive. In a little while he had come to life. They were sitting decorously at opposite sides of the large round table, drinking and talking softly. He had gone to bed and left them there, and since that evening nothing had happened either to increase or diminish his suspicions.

Fully occupied with his own agonies, Dick Coleman could hardly be aware of Jeanette as another person; but he knew she was his wife. He also had a strong feeling that Max was his inferior. Although he was quite prepared to have him in the house, to sit and drink and talk with him and use him as a convenient equerry, all his snobbishness revolted at the thought that he might be making love to his wife. Knowing that Jeanette would be incapable of understanding such a point of view only increased Dick's mistrust of her. At this very moment he only assumed she was asleep in her room; he realized suddenly how little he knew of what went on in the house. With an effort he stood up. The expression on his gaunt face was strained, anguished, and pitiable as he walked slowly into the hall and up the stairs. He was still weak from his stay in the clinic, and weakened further by the effort of sustained thought necessary to carry out his plan.

Facing him on the first floor landing was the door to Jeanette's room. He turned the handle quietly. The large bed stretched smooth and unruffled between him and the window, no indication as to where she might be. Sighing, he withdrew. The next door led to the bathroom, the following to his own room. He passed them both, then looked quickly into the dressing room, but that too was empty. He was now at the end of the hall. On one side a small staircase led up to the servants' quarters, on the other stood the final door, that of a suite of two unused rooms. Already Dick was losing interest; he had almost forgotten what he was looking for. It seemed as if he had been in the corridor forever, as if he had opened the doors of so many empty rooms that he had long ago lost the reason for his search. He was about to turn away when he heard a noise from the supposedly vacant bedrooms. With no attempt at concealment he opened the door, and before fully realizing what it was he saw, had crossed half the room. A couple lay on the unmade bed, paralysed by surprise. Two heads were turned to him, four eyes looked up imploringly. For a moment Dick was as unable to move as they. Then, all three people were released from the spell at the same moment. The man rolled over, sat up, and began babbling nervously. The girl pulled down her skirt and turned to the wall. Dick recognized them to be the cook's son and one of the maids. He could not understand what the man was saying, and knew that he, also, would not be understood. But as he backed away, he said in his high-pitched, drawling, and unreal voice, 'Sorry, I was just looking for my wife.' He stumbled over the hall carpet, and turning around, left the door ajar. Muttering to himself and trembling slightly, he progressed to his own room.

Although it was almost midnight, they had just finished dinner. Jeanette had held up the meal until Joe could leave his bar and Max the hotel. 'Well,' she continued. 'I talked to the man this morning – my God, it was terrible having to see him so early! – and fixed up about the club. That'll be wonderful, won't it, darling?' She was sitting on the floor, leaning against the chair in which Dick slumped, and turned to smile at him, but his sullen gaze did not leave the fire. In no way disconcerted, she nodded to Joe. 'Yes, I've signed all the papers, and so we have it for the summer. We'd better go down there tomorrow to look it over.'

'What the hell are you talking about?' Dick demanded, swinging his head around sharply. 'We're talking about the nightclub, dear, that you're going to run this summer. Don't you remember?' 'Oh, yes, the nightclub.' His mood changed immediately to interest and elation. 'That's wonderful! So you've got it all fixed up? Good! I've always said I'd be good at running a place like that. Don't you think I will, Joe? I get on well with people, and that's the main thing when you have a bar, isn't it?' He was eager for confirmation and approval, for a long, detailed business conversation between professional equals.

'Yes, that's true,' Joe assented, but Dick's brows wrinkled uncertainly trying to assess the depths of his sincerity. 'Oh yes, that's the main thing. If your customers like you then they come back, and before you know where you are you've got a regular crowd.' Max knew his role. He smoothly agreed, while pouring drinks for them all. 'Will you be able to get away from your bar tomorrow, Joe?' Jeanette asked. 'The sooner we can get things straightened out the better.' 'We'll have to see about some entertainers before they're all booked up,' Joe said. 'It's late already.' 'They'll be glad to have the chance to work in my bar,' Dick cut in. 'It'll be the best place on the island.' 'You can't expect Joe to be more interested in your bar than in his own,' Jeanette admonished, laughing; while Joe, a clear film of wariness sliding down over his eyes like the transparent inner lid of an owl, invisible yet changing his attitude to one of alertness and contempt, contradicted her. 'I don't think Dick and I will come into competition,' he said with false joviality. 'He'll have the best bar on his side of the island, and I'll have the best on mine.'

The doorbell cut into their talk, and Max went to answer it. It sounded as if a large party were entering the house, but he led in only four people: an elderly couple, permanent members of the foreign colony and habitués of Joe's bar, retired with petrified livers and opinions from some British protectorate, and two dandified young men, spinning out their post-college grand tour of Europe, already months overdue in their return to the realities awaiting them in some business community of Texas. With the shreds of a gracious colonial manner the woman explained that, having met earlier in the evening over their after-dinner drinks (and presumably boring each other to distraction, although this was a factor she did not mention), they had hit on the alleviating idea of paying the Colemans a visit. The two young men could not wait to tell of an adventure of the early evening. An imperceptive prostitute had tried to pick them up, first singly, then together. 'She must have been really desperate,' one of them giggled. 'And such a luscious creature, too.' 'Absolutely shameful!' the woman trumpeted fiercely. 'Bimbo,' she addressed her husband, a frail-looking man who sat musing over a glass held between mauve-blotched knuckles. 'We'll have to discuss this with the Commandante when we next see him.' 'Yes, of course, dear,' he assented absently, not lifting his head. 'I'm glad to say that such an incident has never taken place in my presence,' she stated. 'It's the fault of the tourists, bringing all this riff-raff into the bars. Those women should be dealt with firmly.' 'They've got to live, too,' Joe said with lazy tolerance.

'This bottle's empty,' Jeanette announced in feigned surprise, holding it up for them to see. 'Is there any more whisky over there?' 'I believe this is brandy I have, my dear,' Bimbo murmured. 'Well, there's plenty of that,' Jeanette smiled. 'We're drinking brandy, too,' the young men chorused. 'So that means we've finished it on our own. How are you doing, Dick? You're not drinking too much, are you?' 'There should be some whisky left – I saw a crate in the kitchen the other day.' Max went to look. 'What do you mean, am I drinking too much?' Dick demanded furiously. 'Do you think I don't know how much I can drink?' 'It's because of what the doctor says –' Jeanette answered, eyelids lowering with the modesty of hopelessness. 'I just don't want you to get sick again.'

This was the moment of choice, in which he could decide whether to be sane or insane; or so it appeared to Dick, suddenly aware of the muted group of people all hoping he would not notice their apprehension. They're watching me as if I were a dangerous animal, he thought without any rancour, and that isn't really the way they should look at their host, is it? Of course Jeanette doesn't want me to drink too much, it's because she loves me, isn't it? Of course, a reassuring voice broke in from further back in his brain. She must love you, look at the way she stays with you. And these people here, they're really very nice, you don't want to frighten them. No, I don't suppose I do, although of course, it would be fun. It would be terrible, another voice took over, the cracked, desperate voice that remembered the drugs and the shocks, the torturing treatments that scaled him down to skeleton. You wouldn't really frighten them, they frighten you more. Don't let them, then. Why should you be frightened? The earlier and more reassuring voice had returned, and he thought that this time he would really listen to it. He could feel his resolution, his calmness, distilling more surely every moment, and was glad he had escaped, even if only for a short respite, the terrifying and exhausting necessity to be mad.

'I know, sweetheart, I know,' he muttered. Dimly aware of his swoop away from them all, Jeanette became suddenly animated. 'Where is that drink?' she asked no one in particular, and as if in reply, Max pushed through the door from the kitchen with a bottle of whisky in each hand. 'These are the only two I could find,' he announced. 'Well, there's enough for me now, anyway,' Jeanette replied.

Max's sudden entrance brought up to the surface of Dick's mind all those doubts concerning that young man's relationship with Jeanette which he had been trying to forget. His effort towards self-control had left him incapable of another one immediately. Fear and insecurity screamed down and clamped their talons into the back of his neck, irritating and blinding him by the beating of their wings and the scratch of their feathers, choking him with their rank smell, completely enveloping his head as they strained their necks around to get at his eyes. 'Get away!' he shouted, flailing long thin arms to drive them off. The glass he was holding dropped to the tiled floor, and surprisingly did not break. 'Get them off me,' he begged. The elderly English couple and the two young men looked towards Jeanette uneasily, then to Max and Joe, then back again at him. They were embarrassed, curious, and faintly afraid, but Dick felt no pity or sympathy in them. 'Get them out of here,' he shouted. This direct attack explained his earlier, mystifying pleas and exorcised momentarily the unseen presences which had disturbed them.

'I think it would be best if we went, my dear,' the Englishwoman said. 'Oh Dick, what's the matter?' Jeanette implored, reaching to touch his arm, and turning to her guests confusedly. 'Shall I call the doctor?' Max asked, while the Texans edged away from the group formed by Dick with Jeanette holding one arm and Joe ready by his side to take the other. Bimbo remained seated, his glass twirling reflectively but forgotten in his old hands. 'Get them off me, get them away from my head,' Dick screamed again, lunging away from Jeanette with a movement that broke her grasp and made those nearest take one involuntary step backwards. 'Come along dear, I'm sure Mrs Coleman would rather we go.' The Englishwoman picked up her bag and marshalled her eager ranks. 'I do hope that everything will be all right,' she called sweetly over her shoulder as she entered the safety of the hall. 'Don't bother to show us out, we'll find the way. I can see you're much too busy.' With an inappropriate smile bestowed impartially on the room, she shut them in and was gone.

'We'd better get him upstairs,' Jeanette grimly directed. 'Yes, I think we should get hold of the *practicante*, anyway,' she replied to Max. 'He'll need a shot of something.' Relieved to be out of the eye of the cyclone, Max picked up the phone. 'Come along upstairs, sweetheart,' Jeanette murmured. 'Come and lie down.' If he lay down, nothing could tear at the back of his neck. Disdaining any help from Joe, but taking the arm Jeanette offered, against which he leaned so heavily that she could barely support his weight, they passed through the hall and up the dimly lit stairs to his room. He was one of the mainstays of the *practicante*'s monthly income, so the man soon arrived on his motor-bike and knocked him out with an injection. Afterwards he accepted a drink from Jeanette but not her invitation to stay, then left her in front of the fire, talking worriedly of what she could do about Dick.

Lunch hour had emptied the beach. Along its gritty margin were signs that people had been there a short time ago, and around the curve of the bay, against the powdery insubstantiality of the foothills in the noon light, the newly-built hotels could not quite contain the sounds of those tourists nor the hot oily smell of the meals they were eating. A particularly strong puff of frying meat reached Dick where he sat in solitary possession. He grimaced with distaste, stood up, and moved further away. Bleached cream boxer shorts made his lean body seem as dark as an Indian's. Beach life suited him; he sweated out enough alcohol to keep sober. Among the reddening holiday-makers he appeared to be nothing more alarming than a misanthropic and sun-obsessed eccentric. He lay on the stones, stalked back and forth from the bar for a drink, sometimes went into the sea, and had not been so healthy for years.

The bar was too big, the rent was too high, and for the sake of the wholesaler's commission Joe had overstocked it. The tourists who were brought down in groups every two weeks were not the sort of people for whom the bar had been planned. They did not want to go back to drink night after night. One visit to the Club Flamingo and a bottle of Spanish champagne was a nice change, but something in the atmosphere made them uneasy. So the dancers danced and the guitarist strummed to the two or three occupied tables, while from one corner of the room Dick watched them sardonically, drank methodically, then more often than not went early to bed. When Jeanette came over he would put on a shirt and a pair of trousers, and silently ignore the discussions about business. His interest and enthusiasm had been exhausted even before arrival. As far as he was concerned, the pretence she and Joe still kept up about him being in control was a farcical waste of time.

People were coming onto the beach again, mostly those young and energetic ones who did not take a siesta. Although the sun was high, they wanted to throw balls to each other and shout; and there were always a couple pumping their legs up and down mechanically on a pedalo. Their return was the signal that it was time for his meal, and he walked up to the road and across the tram-track to the bar. When he was almost there, he saw a figure which immediately put him on guard. In a pair of white trousers pressed into military perfection, and a brass-buttoned blue linen blazer that far outdid in elegance the clients of the luxury hotel where he worked, Max was seated in the shade of the doorway. That meant Jeanette was present on one of her tours of inspection, that he would have to spend the rest of the day in their company. Instead of the dark peace of the sun he would be in the confusing gloom of the bar in daylight; the familiar emptiness of his existence was going to be filled with talk and people.

'Hello, Dick,' Max called as he sighted him. 'Here comes the manager,' he grinned over his shoulder to Joe and Jeanette who were talking near the back of the bar. Jeanette smiled distractedly. The overstocking had made her angry, but now Joe had carried his effrontery even further. Crates of drink were missing. It was obvious he had taken them to his own bar. The two waiters, eating at one of the empty tables, listened indifferently to their tense voices. 'Hello, Jeanette,' Dick said. He wondered for a moment if she were getting thinner. He had become used to the tanned bodies of the girls who ran up and down the beach all day around him; in comparison Jeanette looked pale and slack and tired. Her light dress was creased from the journey and her skin seemed damp, as if the heat were too much. 'You look well, Dick,' she said. Walking over from his seat by the door, Max added, 'Yes, this life of responsibility seems to suit him.' Dick answered aggressively, 'Yes, it does suit me. Let's have a drink, Joe. Come on, all of you, have it on me. Have it on the house.'

Listlessly they sat down. No mention was made of lunch. Dick was the one who talked. By virtue of his almost naked body he seemed to dominate them. The others were glad to remain silent. They were lulled by the afternoon gloom and the unexpected relief of seeing him so well into not noticing how much he was drinking.

Some slight gesture or remark of Max's changed everything. 'So you've come here for your day in the country!' Dick shouted, rearing up from his chair. Alarmed and uncomprehending, they saw him pour the half bottle of brandy over Max's white trousers. 'How dare you come here with my wife, wearing those trousers!' He scooped their glasses from the table and hurled them to the floor. His dark, thin body making these violent movements did not seem human. He leaped over the bar and plucked bottles from the shelves, throwing them wild. The waiters withdrew rapidly, as did Max, furious about his ruined trousers. Joe and Jeanette were left to hear him cursing them, cursing the birds at his neck that would not leave him alone, and cursing the insult of the white trousers until everything was wrecked. He was exhausted by then, his torso slippery with sweat and marked by blood where broken glass had scratched him. Jeanette crouched on the wet floor and held his head against her.

The sound of voices took her to the top of the stairs. Max had just come in and was talking to the cook's son. 'How are you getting on with Catalina?' The boy giggled proudly. 'You'd better not stain the mattresses,' Max continued, poking him in the side. 'How did you manage it? You're the lucky one, having a nice young girl like that. She looks the loving type, eh?' The phone rang from a downstairs room but neither answered it. She shouted, 'Max, answer the phone.' 'Oh, all right,' he called, moving reluctantly. 'It's probably only the clinic,' he muttered in an irritated undertone, but she heard him, and afraid that he would not trouble to find out anything, clattered down the stairs to take the call herself.

The daily report on Dick's condition was that he was well, there was no change. A new treatment kept him subdued and listless, and he had even gained some weight. He no longer complained about his food or his bed when she went to see him; he had nothing to say at all. 'I suppose he's the same,' Max said. 'Yes, what do you expect?' she answered hotly. 'Do you want him to get worse?' 'No, not really.' 'I suppose you'd like him to die?' she demanded, pressing to get some sort of response. 'Goodness, no. Do you think I want to marry you?' 'I'm not that much of a fool,' she said bitterly. 'That's right,' he agreed. 'I don't want any encumbrances.' He must have thought better of the sentence he seemed about to add, for he stopped, changed his tone of voice, and continued, 'Now Jeanette, don't be angry, sweetheart. I know it always makes you nervous when you hear from the clinic. Let's have a drink, or do you want to go out?' 'What do you want to do? You've just come in,' she asked, smiling and putting a hand on his shoulder. 'Do you feel like going out again right away?' Masterfully he opted for remaining at home.

'Let's have a party tonight,' he said after downing his first drink. Jeanette did not respond with the alacrity she might have shown the previous spring. Since Max had moved into the house she thought it had served as the setting for far too many parties. 'We can't just sit here staring at each other,' he said threateningly. 'Sure, sure, good idea,' Jeanette agreed. 'Who do you want to phone?' He suggested a list of people, including Joe's name. 'No, I won't have him here,' she said firmly. 'You know that. Why do you keep trying?' 'I'm only fooling you, Jeanette.' He laughed, delighted to have made her lose her temper.

The tourist season ended before the Bar Flamingo had covered the money spent on its opening. Their final accounting revealed that Joe had cheated her even more than she had allowed for. She wanted to break with him entirely, but Max would not allow it. 'I have business of my own with him,' he said. 'But he really cheated me,' Jeanette reiterated. 'Don't you understand? I hate the bastard.' 'It doesn't matter,' Max replied. 'I've still got to keep on good terms with him.' He declined to explain more, but from time to time asserted his power by sitting her down at Joe's bar while he and Joe retired to a back room to do whatever it was that constituted this business.

'All right, then, I won't phone Joe,' Max assured her. 'There'll be enough people anyway.' 'This place is a mess with all these parties,' Jeanette said dubiously. 'Well, why don't you have it cleaned up?' he asked. Max had given up his supervision of the domestic staff, but the slight control

Jeanette had previously had was undermined entirely by his presence. The only work that seemed to go on was the continual cooking of enormous and elaborate meals for the servants, and the provisioning this involved. Now and then two plates of food got as far as the dining room, but more often Jeanette found herself grubbing in a larder of leftovers, the remains of meals she had never seen, smelled, or tasted, slicing up ends of what obviously had been large roasts of meat in order to make a few sandwiches. The bills were enormous, but in the confusion and flux of the household, and the chaotic melancholy of her daily life, food bills seemed too unimportant to concern her. The whole house needed cleaning, all surfaces were filmed with dust. Max's room was like that of an adolescent prostitute. Jeanette had learned that his impeccable appearance bore no relationship to the setting in which it was achieved. Apart from the food which every day one or other of the servants took home, linen and clothes were vanishing. When Dick went to the clinic she put his things away, but half the dirty shirts upstairs belonged to him, had been worn by Max and then pushed into the bottom of his closet, or perhaps by the cook's son, she had no way of knowing. That afternoon she had spent almost an hour looking for a blouse. The search had been unsuccessful. Like bracelets, stockings, Dick's winter underwear, and her own ideas about the future, it had vanished.

Max and Joe's business was currency. Jeanette knew that Max could get her a better rate than anyone else, but was not aware of Joe's part in these transactions. Most of Dick's income was consumed by medical expenses, but Jeanette's mother had left her enough investments to live even at her present wasteful rate. Cheques arrived at three-monthly intervals. On Max's suggestion, the last two had been sent direct to her rather than through a bank. Both times he had returned them in the form of piles of soft, creased bank notes, unbelievable money that seemed to have no connection with the thin slip of paper he had taken, the spending of which could never be a serious thing. She offered him the current cheque immediately. 'It's a bit tricky just now,' he said. 'You'd better keep it a few days.'

It was more money than the other times, almost five thousand dollars. It would of course need some arranging for him and Joe to get hold of that much currency, but this was not the reason Max refused it. He wanted time to think about what he was going to do, to be sure that this really was the opportunity he had been waiting for, the moment to move and act when hesitation would only result in fatal regret. He was finished with Jeanette. He felt sure he could remain in his present job forever, or get another at any hotel in the world. But with more than five thousand dollars, for he had money saved also, everything would be different; he would take on the role of a master. So the thoughts thrummed through his brain for the next two days while the decision was being made. The same timorousness that had stopped him seducing Jeanette was the cause of his hesitation, and the memory of how she had led him up to her bed made him gloat at the thought of stealing her money.

Even before admitting to himself what he would do, Max was planning the practical details. If he could manage it without Joe's help, with Joe not even aware that Max had flown until hearing it as a piece of gossip some days later, so much the better. Joe had always been too condescending, had joked too many times about his eager and badly concealed ambitiousness. He might either betray him or want some of the money himself in order not to do so. So Max prepared his disappearance very carefully. It was a good thing he had left the hotel, because to remove his few possessions from Jeanette's house would be easier than running the gauntlet of lift-boys, waiters, chambermaids, clerks and even friendly clients while passing through halls and reception rooms. The disorder of the villa allowed much more freedom. After weighing up the different advantages of the various methods he could think of, he decided to deposit the cheque in a Swiss bank, and use only money he had quite legitimately saved for his cash in hand. And where would he go? The whole world was there to choose from: for a start he would spend a couple of weeks in Paris.

He was surprised at how sentimental he felt at leaving Jeanette, once the decision was made. It even crossed his mind that he might miss her. But she had become too melancholy; a sadness not caused by him and thus belittling. The hard and confident woman he had seen in her and who had fascinated him had become a source of uneasiness. She was too difficult, so deserved to be abandoned. The superstructure of imagination had shrivelled and collapsed, and nothing else could exist on that burnt territory. Taking her money would strip away the final shreds of what had captivated him. By the time he had settled the matter in his own mind Jeanette's cheque had been sent off, his savings converted into francs and dollars, and his travelling wardrobe, which included a few items of Dick's, safely conveyed out of the house. He would have liked to say something which would serve as a farewell, a few sentences whose significance she would only understand later. But nothing sufficiently allusive occurred to him; he was afraid he might give himself away. He left the house one morning when Jeanette was still asleep, collected his month's salary, and full of fear and excitement took a cab to the airport.

The storms that autumn went on and on; it seemed to Jeanette they had begun the day Max left, became even worse as she realized he had swindled her, then settled into a steady, downpouring monotony. She hardly went out except for the daily visit to Dick, but sat in the gloom of the salon before an ineffectual fire drinking slowly through bottle after bottle of whatever liquor was brought. For three days she had made no move to find where Max had gone, so that when she did report the matter to the police, he really had vanished. She wrote to her brokers for more money, and after these efforts settled back into lethargic indifference. Then one morning the sky was clear. It was a shock to wake to such blueness and see shadows again; she had expected to be able to drift on forever in the same grey sadness of rain.

As she left Dick's room a nurse asked if she had time to see the director. 'Your husband seems to be in a calm period, *señora*. If nothing disturbs him it should continue. Are you planning to remain in this city?' His direct question made her realize she had no plans at all. The events of the year marshalled themselves into high, shining, unjointed walls that diminished backwards and led forward to embarkation. 'Of course, my husband's illness has kept me here,' she answered quickly. 'If I thought he could travel –' 'You must know about his illness by now,' he said, forcing one side-piece of his glasses back over and over again, as if it were too long, or as if once a pair had been badly fitting and since then he had never lost the habit. 'No one can say when he will be really ill again, and of course he is not a well man, nor will he ever be one. But I think you could travel with him. If you did it slowly, he might enjoy it.' 'Well, I'd prefer to fly,' she mused. 'But there'll be a lot of luggage – it would probably be better to go by boat. When can he leave?' 'Whenever you wish,' the director replied, pushing the heavy glasses up his nose, his voice colder. 'Well, he can come right now.' She would be glad to have him home, in spite of what this severe-looking Spaniard might think.

Dick fumbled among the remaining items of his wardrobe trying to help Jeanette to pack, as little use as a young child and just as touching in his efforts. When the house was clear of the things she had bought at various times in an attempt to make it more comfortable, the damage to the walls and furniture showed up even more. One morning she went over it with the agent while he listed the repairs and replacements to be made. His previous experience of renting furnished houses to foreigners had made him expect a fight. He had been prepared to argue about each separate item, and felt disappointed to be deprived of one of the more subtle gratifications of his work. Jeanette agreed to everything. Money would plaster all wounds and walls.

The cook, the cook's son, and the two maids, in a glycerine sea of parting tips and bonuses, were as emotional as old family retainers while she said good-bye. Tall, pale, and ghostly, Dick echoed her farewells. Jeanette also was pale as they got into the taxi; it had been hard work clearing up the house and packing, arranging all the irritating details of their departure. She had drunk too much and not slept enough, and had lost more weight. Her face seemed slacker and older. All the bars were lit up as they drove past them on their way to the night ferry, and through the misted glass of the taxi and the bar windows she thought she could see some of the people who had come to those many parties. When they arrived at the quay it was raining again. She took Dick's arm as he shuffled up the gangway to the boat and their cabin.

Frederick Busch

and something is moving

just under the skin
and they know
that it is not blood.

from 'The Move'
by James Tate

Something is Moving Just Under the Skin

I think again tonight of Rogovin – I say, 'Good night'. I say, 'Good-bye, go win the war – because the *ratchet* that our bed heaved, going *ratchet*, going *ratchet*, going *ratchet*, was the same steel music that the elevator played in U.S.A.F.E.E.S. New York, its khaki corridors, the steel of its slamming doors, when Rogovin and all of us were pale and much too loud or soft, and waited for the army doctors on their long floor. You make the room warm when you sleep, and I am saying this to you because you know my name and Rogovin is leaving now, without my name or voice or phlegm-burned breath remembered, and he won't recall them, or the paleness of my gums, the moisture of the fingertips I stumbled with to take his matchbook while the *ratchet* of the hung cage descending in the well of those national stairs creaked morning in.

There was a smell of last night's floorwash of ammonia and a yellow on the ceiling from the underpowered bulbs. A small fast man in military blue brought coffee in a paper cup and watched us watch him drink it. And we sat on wooden benches, staring as the coffee disappeared, and waiting for the sermon to begin. He rubbed at his freckled face and asked a hundred of us, 'how the hell early can you get?' and listened to the chorus coming in: shoes rubbing on the vinyl floor, a scrape of elbows over wood, low hum. He smiled and lit a cigarette, sat on a table and swung his legs; he spread his short arms out and told us, 'Men –'

'No smoking.'

'That,' said the one with the cigarette, 'is how the army works.' He pointed to a side door and not much more than five feet of vertical creases, green, and said, 'They treat you that way. Join the air force.'

The one at the door said, 'And napalm the *civil*ians?' He put one finger into the top of his crewcut and told us, 'Smoke your sleepy civilian heads right off, men, puff it up everybody light *up*: you work that cancer up big, blow it up big now, you can stay home awhile, get the pick of the women. *Light* up.'

'Men,' said the one in blue, 'there will be no smoking on the examination floor due to military requirements and not to mention fire laws.' He looked straight into us and said, 'I would advise you now to grab a smoke while there is still time.' He pointed again to the side door now empty, waved his legs back and forth and smiled and told us, 'I'll take care of them.'

Smoke went up like flies in a field, and boys in shiny pants uninjuredly limped, waved their heads, shouted over the benches and the smoke: 'Hey Petronis. Petronis! Hey: Petronis!'

'Ho Duke.'

'Petronis, you joined up?'

'Hey Duke!'

'You joining up?'

'Scratch my titty, will ya?'

'You joining up?'

'Where's the kid?'

'They called you down, huh?'

'The kid get a letter too?'

'Who?'

'Hey, I'll see ya later, right? Duke? Catch me after, right?'

'Yo.'

There were grins the sounds of furniture moving, the *ratchet* of the elevator outside in the centre of the double stairs. The fat boy next to me said, 'Here goes matches.'

'Excuse me?'

'Matches. You looked like you needed some matches. You want some?'

'Oh! Yeah, yes, thank you. Thanks a lot.'

'Watch it,' he said. 'Forget it, here we go, kill the smoke.'

Another short one in green stood at the front of the room and took a stack of brown envelopes from the one in blue and then called out, 'No smoking. Butts out. Let's go.' I stood up and he said, 'Take your seat. Resume seating, there. Move only upon my clearly feasible command.'

The fat boy next to me said, 'Duffy of San Quentin, that's old Duffy, I had him here the last time. Tweet-tweet.'

I put my cigarette gently on the floor and gently suffocated it, while the fat boy said, 'This your first time,' and I nodded. 'Start working up a piss,' he said. 'And don't talk too much, they hate it when you talk. But scared? Look scared? Everybody's your mother right away, love-love, just look scared and try not talking. Right? I know the bit, the whole thing, watch the way I move it.'

'I'm a married man,' I said.

'Don't work, they take those now. You four-eff?'

'I don't know.'

'No, I mean the class, you know. What they classify you?'

'Two-ess.'

'You go to school?'

'Full-time.'

'You're clear, why'd you come here? You don't have to do the bit. Go home.'

'They told me to come, I came. That's the way it works.'

'You got the letter and you go to school? Why'd you get the letter? Jesus, they got all the spastics running this thing you don't have to *be* here. You know that?' His fat fingers, knuckles black, ran figures on the air. 'You don't,' he said. 'It's okay, you don't have to sweat a thing, I'll tell you who to talk to at the end, but do the bit, they don't listen till you do the bit. You just hang in and work the piss up, run through the zoo parade, I'll tell you who to talk to later.'

'Hey-oh!' Duffy told us what it meant. 'Re-sume silence, men, we are about to commence.'

'I had him the two last times,' the fat boy whispered. 'Every time they marked me down fat, he personally right away got pissed off. He's very serious about being fat.' He pushed the sleeve of my loden coat and I turned around. 'You're not too fat, you know? You can't make it that way but it's okay. Don't talk, look scared: I'll get you through the bit.'

I waved my nose toward Duffy and the fat boy pushed my sleeve and said, 'My name is Rogovin,' and pointed, hand held low, to the front of the room. 'Catch the Beast of Budapest bit.'

'And also to help you,' Duffy was telling us. 'Far from filling a local quota, and far from making sure nobody succeeds in the evadence of his righteous civil duties, and not only to carry on the law – that's, ah, not the only *thing*.' He looked me in the eye. I closed my eyes. 'Do you see what I'm saying men? You have to get this now: far from, ah. That, *all* of that now. Some of you are *sick*.

'Now. Look around you.' The benches rocked, squeaked, as the boys looked around, as the elevator ran in place, as the cold floor trembled to the subway underneath. 'Some of you are *sick* and you don't know that. But I'm telling you the justifiable truth. We know, we know how to find out and *cure* you so that you *can* take all of your places, ever last man in this room. In the service of your country. That's right. If you have cancer and don't know it, we have ways of finding out, and so forth, heart disease, cataracts, obesity, the whole gambit of physical unrest.

'So. Why are you here so early on a Monday morning?' He held his hand spread wide, for us to see. '*First*, duty to your country.' The thumb curled away. 'Following of the laws, ah, you must follow.' His index finger knuckled in behind the thumb. 'Self-help if you are ignorant of one or more diseases you may or may not have.' His middle finger folded on the thumb and the remaining two tilted forward, wavered, dropped, then, into a hanging fist we watched.

'*There*fore, you will come to this desk upon receiving your name to pick up *one* envelope of that same name and *two* New York City subway tokens constituting carfare reimbursement travelling to and from this area. *Pro*ceed.'

And then the two of them, Duffy in green, the other one in blue, called off a hundred names and got a hundred answers and one hundred envelopes, physical questionnaires clipped outside, were carried on the vinyl floors through green hallways to the double stairs that climbed around the elevator shaft like wide and darkened marble vines. I patted for my wallet, then my keys, my loose change. I pulled at the hem of my coat, pushed the clip on the envelope, sniffed at the cold recollection of dust that the lights gave.

Rogovin said, 'Don't *sweat* it, I'm telling you this is no sweat. I had this bit four times, no pain.'

'Just work the piss up,' I said.

'Listen, everybody goes through here, they don't care about you, they just want to get your ass out. They're in a hurry. No sweat. Look: you're a doctor. Right? You come here, no dough for it, and you stand up there all day and look for piles. Right? How particular you get? Right? And you don't even have to *be* here, Jesus, don't worry. Look: you want some help, you know, I'll get you through, what the hell. Okay?'

'Is the whole thing naked?'

'Huh?'

'When do we strip?'

'Oh, they get you down pretty fast. Why? You like that stuff?'

'I mean, do they let you keep anything on?'

'What, you don't like it? Or you do?'

'I don't care.'

'No, I mean it.'

'I don't care.'

'You ever read a book called *Blonde Girl's Buff*? Detective book? They put it out in paperback.'

'No, I –'

'I read a lot. I don't have too much time, you know? So I can't see dying in front of the teevee, I read. Not like you, but I like it.'

'No, no, I read detective books, I like them a lot.'

'Ever read *Blonde Girl's Buff*?'

'No, I think I missed it. I'll check in the library, though, you really recommend it.'

'I don't remember who wrote the thing but they got a strip scene in there? Jesus.'

On the third floor we walked along a balcony that surrounded the stairs that surrounded the elevator. No one shouted in that unlighted landing, but Rogovin chanted off the signs on doors we passed, calling 'Visual Examination', 'Feet', 'Audial Perception', until I breathed to the rhythm of his words. Whoever led us walked into a small room filled with chairs. A short Negro in green watched us through black-rimmed glasses and, when everyone had sat, he snapped his fingers.

'That,' he called in a high voice, 'is the sound you will respond to henceforth. Which means from now on in case you are not an educated individual.' He snapped again. 'That means look at me and shape up and do as I tell you.' He snapped again. 'Do not fail to hang onto every syllable I form.'

He snapped. 'I am coming among you to leave off army-issue pencils and I will not release this muster until each pencil is accounted for.' He came among us and left us pencils and a smell of coffee that made my mouth dry, the sides of my head feel thin. Then he snapped his fingers and we focused on his mouth, the pale lips cutting with precision in the small cold room of chairs. 'You are now to fill in the questionnaire printed in brown ink. Noting the large chart on the blackboard, using it as an example, you should have no difficulty, but I will help you free civilians through the first few questions starting *now*.'

He snapped. 'Name first.' He folded his hands in front of his crotch and sighed. 'Who does not know his name?' He looked at the back of the room and nodded his head, 'Your name is *sheeit*. Is that clear? Good. Who else?'

He snapped. 'Number two calls for race. The army does not care for the fine distinctions and you will therefore enter Caucasian if you are white, Negro if you are black, Mongolian if you are tan, and Vietcong if you are either pinto or palomino.'

Snap: 'Respiratory defects will be answered as follows.' Snap: 'T.B. is most interesting and will be treated in the following way.' Snap: 'Note the bedwetting question. I am certain some of you will have to answer yes.' Snap: 'Spitting blood.' Snap: 'Motion-sickness.' Snap: 'Diarrhoea.' Snap:

'Orthopaedic has to do with bones.' Snap: 'Night-sweats.' Snap: 'Upset stomach.' Snap: 'Urinary pain.' Snap: 'Any kind of ulcer.' Snap: 'Recent loss of weight.' Snap: 'Dizziness at heights.' Snap: 'Claustrophobic symptoms.' Snap: 'Frequency of headaches.' Snap: 'Numbness of the limbs.' Snap: 'Scarlet fever.' Snap: 'Jaundice.' Snap: 'Smallpox.' Snap: 'Measles.' Snap: 'Mumps.' Snap: 'Fits.' Snap: 'Death.'

Snap: 'I said who here has had a case of *death*?' The glasses looked us over. 'You ain't dead, civilians. You are just lying down on this very very easy job and *playing* dead. And' – snap – 'you will therefore sign your names at the bottom of the sheet and give me those army-issue pencils back and leave me be.' He snapped his fingers and came among us and we gave him the pencils to count and he waved us away.

Rogovin walked up beside me as the group – was someone leading us, did someone know where all of us were meant to be each time we moved? – was eaten by the darkness at the doorway of the small room with chairs. 'I tell you?' he said. 'Like a machine, they never know you're there. I'll get you through.'

'Would you carry aspirin around with you? Would you please have about eighteen aspirin I could borrow for a couple of minutes?'

'You don't have a headache,' he said.

'Now, that's a relief, Rogovin. You know, I was walking up these stairs and thinking I had this totally ferocious headache until you told me how silly I was to believe it. That's my trouble: every time my head hurts very badly I think I have a headache, I know it's silly. Thank you for your help.'

'You're only scared.'

'What?'

'You're scared. It's all it is, I had it the first time through.

You know, you keep feeling like all of a sudden they grab you and put you in a truck and put you in a plane and you're in a land war in Asia and your wife's home crying, it's all over, you're through. Right? Okay. Except there's enough guys to get without you and me and they don't *want* you. And you're not supposed to be here anyway. Right? So make believe you're not here.'

The elevator, clanging in the shaft, going *ratchet* through the stairs, was on the fifth floor waiting, and there was Duffy too, in green: 'Form up, men. Two lines, coats and ties off, right sleeves rolled high, coats and envelopes carried in the left hand, *pro*ceed.'

We walked around a large room filled with chairs and cots, the room so brightly lighted that I squinted, squeezed my temples, looked from the light wooden floor and folding furniture to the wall, where a black sign said in white letters THE MEN ARE IN THE ARMY NOW/ THEY'RE BUSY/DO YOU WANT TO WAIT 'TIL THEY COME BACK?/OR WOULD YOU LIKE TO JOIN THEM?/ . . . IF YOU'RE GOOD ENOUGH. I looked back to the room, at the cloth partition against the rear wall. A voice behind the cloth called, 'Okay, Ralph' and Duffy waved the boys at the head of the line inside.

Someone behind me whispered, 'Confession' but no one laughed, no one spoke – except Rogovin, who told us, 'Little blood sample, no sweat, you don't even feel it.'

A tall blond boy in front of us, white shirt transparent with sweat, slapped at a chair and it collapsed against the pale glossy floor like a stiff man dying.

Duffy called out, 'You like to break things up? We can use you in a country I heard about. You pick that blackass chair up and stand it upright parallel to the ground and *re*sist from fooling around this-*forth*. Is that clear?'

The blond boy rubbed his hands on his thighs and said, 'I wasn't tooling around.'

The line moved up towards the partition. Rogovin tripped and fell like a filled-in gong, saying, as he swayed on his knees like something rung, 'He's humping the whole thing up, he's humping it up.'

Duffy was there, telling the blond boy, 'I said *fooling* sonny, I didn't say a word about *tooling*, and you will *not* instigate words in my mouth. Co-*rect*?'

The line moved up. The boy said, 'No sir.'

'Because that places you in dire ah doesn't it?'

'Yes, sir.'

'Okay. Now. What's your complaint?'

'Sir.'

'The problem. We're running out of *time*. What's the problem with you?'

A boy in loose brown pants walked from the other side of the curtain, his forearm at a right angle to his biceps, a vial of dark blood in the high hand. He rolled his eyes back and smiled at the line. The line moved up. The blond boy said, 'Can I get out of giving blood, sir? I can't do it, I get sick, I faint.'

'You a hermaphrodite, you bleed too much, you carry a card?'

'No, sir. I get sick.'

'From *what*?'

'From giving blood.' The line moved up. 'I get sick when I do it, I can't do it.'

'Learn it, it's a thing you have to know how to do.'

'I'm not gonna do it, sir.' The blond boy spread his feet and Duffy tensed on his toes, crouched. 'I'm not. I'll get a letter from a doctor, I'll come back this afternoon but I'm not gonna do it. Please.'

'Hump the whole thing,' Rogovin said. 'Screw us all.

You see?' he said to me. '*That's* what gets you screwed, when you bunch the line up like that, they hate it. That's when the shit flies, you watch.'

Duffy, still on his toes, moved in. Someone behind the partition shouted 'Ralph' and someone at the end of the line sneezed.

Duffy called, 'I got him, it's okay, he's mine,' and he moved in low, chopped his foot down with a long stride and, screaming 'Kiyat*ah*!' reached for the blond boy's arm, pivoted, fell with the arm on his chest, the boy on top of the arm, and was pinned.

'We're finished,' Rogovin said. 'This is it, we'll stay here all the humping *night*.'

The boy stood up and said to Duffy, on the floor, 'You did that, I didn't touch you. Everybody saw that. You tried to throw me, I didn't touch you with my hand, you're not allowed to kick us around.'

Duffy, on his back, looked at the boy, moved one leg slowly, then planted it in the blond boy's crotch. The boy went down like a folding chair and Duffy pulled him up by the hair, held him until his eyes opened, then pushed to his knees, back onto his heels, held his head down. 'Move the line,' he said, panting with clear regularity, 'continue this operation rapidly.'

'Tweet-tweet,' said Rogovin. 'We're screwed.'

I walked behind the partition, sat on a stool and closed my eyes. 'You can open them,' someone said, but I kept them shut and, by the time I had whinnied in pain, I was walking to a chair, holding my blood aloft, watching the line move up and the vial-haulers emerging and then others, rested, handing in their blood to a white-coated, hairless man near the door of the bright room that smelled somehow of vinegar, then leaving with the fist clenched at right angles to the biceps, Duffy and the soundless gagging boy behind them on their knees. I walked slowly to turn in my blood, left slowly for the dark and chilly hall around the elevator shaft, moved slowly with the other scratching shoes so that Rogovin, his shallow breath, his tongue of swift phrases, could catch up and caution me that we were not screwed.

He panted in behind me as the feet were moving down the stairs, he said 'We're screwed.'

Someone in the darkness chattered 'Hey, the big guy says we go get screwed now.' Someone else laughed. No one answered anybody, then, while the elevator winched up slowly from below us to above.

'Rogovin,' I whispered, 'how am I supposed to stay calm if you go pessimistic on me?'

'You can talk out loud,' he said. 'It's only when the rough guys are around, you know, drop it down a little so it's like you're not around. But here? Listen –'

'Rogovin, you sounded panicky before, twenty seconds ago, up on the top of the stairs. What's the story? Do we cool this thing or not? When do I start to worry?'

'Listen, look: don't sweat it. Okay? I know the bit, in-out, tweet-tweet, they give us lunch, we go home. And you don't even have to be here, for chrissakes. Don't sweat, I'll show you what to do.'

'Tweet-tweet.'

'You got it, that's the way the whole thing goes, alright.'

'Where do we have to go now?'

'Third floor, physical exam, men's underpants, ladies' bloomers, underarm deodorants and fine furniture, step down, keep your –'

'This is where we strip?'

'Well they got to *look* at you, right? How they supposed to check us out? Right? Yeah, we take it off, they got the coldest damn floors.'

'Great, I love this, I really love this because I like to suffer so much. Rogovin. Rogovin? What'd you mean, before, upstairs. When you said we were screwed? Did you mean that?'

'I can't do a goddam thing if you panic, you know that? Panic and I can't help. You never heard a figure of speech before.'

'All the time.'

'Okay: so?'

'Tweet-tweet.'

'Rah-toe.'

Someone turned the lights on, then, and sent some heat up, and the little room, its many doors, shelved window, wall of hooks, turned on as if a bulb beneath each board were hot and friendly, and as if the day were given, now, a second chance. Of course Duffy was there, smoking, and so half of us dived for the cigarettes while he watched us listen in our new heat to naked feet, someplace, moving.

'There is no smoking on the examination floor.'

'This is a very unconventional day,' Rogovin said. 'I never saw him here.'

The big Negro in white jacket rubbed his chin and looked at Duffy and, dropping his voice again, said, his chest said, 'We do not smoke on the test floor.'

'I would love to stand up, then and finish it,' came from high-heeled boots and light blue corduroys and a thin wrist wrapped in a silver chain. 'May I do that?'

The big Negro looked at Duffy and Duffy looked at the shelved window. The Negro looked at the floor and said, 'You extinguish the *fag* right now or I find a fire extinguisher and freeze your lips with it to the back of your highly swish mouth in about two seconds, son. Do you see what I mean?'

He backed into a door marked MEN and, when it was half-open, faced into it and went inside. The wrist in silver chain called out, 'I hope you drown, you big black bastard. I'm a ci*vil*ian.'

'Death,' said Rogovin. 'The queers are screwing us all.'

'Men,' said Duffy. 'This has not started out well and I want to give you some advice: shape up. That's all. Get squared away and shape up. Is that *clear*?

'Now. Upon my clearly feasible command you will derobe to one sock and undershorts, leaving all other garments at the window to your direct right, carrying all jewellery and valuables in one sock gripped in the right hand and brown envelope in the left. Upon turning in suitable garments you will proceed. Through *that* door to get weighed and there will be no loud jokes about getting weighed. Good.

'*Is* that clear? As soon as the gentleman at the scales informs you to proceed, you will do so, refraining from all conversation and jesting in order to render yourselves open to sudden commands or pertaining questions. Okay. Good. *Pro*ceed derobing.'

'Rogovin,' I said, but he was gone, prying shoes off with his toes, simultaneously unbuttoning his shirt and yanking at his belt: a thick-fleshed flower throbbing pale from a bud of wool. By the time I had my trousers on a hanger taken from the wall, Rogovin was female breasts unhaired and yellow rolls of goose-bump hung on the whiteness of his brief shorts. A smell of skin went up like smoke and nearly naked Rogovin, racing past the fag in shorts of blue, was diving, almost, through the fog to turn his clothing in and be discovered as obese.

I walked slowly to the clothing window, flexing my feet carefully, trying not to shake or roll, then went into the weighing room. Rogovin was on the giant scales when I got there, and I hoisted my sock to say hello, but he was looking at the dial and saying 'That thing's off, sir. Could that be possible? That it goes under? You know, shows too little, something like that. I don't care – you know, but I got obesed last time and I didn't cut down a thing. You know? I *know* that.'

The Puerto Rican boy in white jacket wrote on Rogovin's physical form, gave it back to him, said, 'You too fat, but you not too too fat. We cahn use you foh a spay tahir if a truck break dohn, nayxt. Good-bye, too-fat, hey I say *nayxt*.'

'No,' Rogovin said, 'you can't just do it that way.' He climbed from the scales, reading his form, shaking his head. 'No,' he said. 'Look, who's your boss? Can I talk to the C.O.? Somebody like that? You can't just do that.'

The Puerto Rican waved his hand and Rogovin stood, legs apart, sock in one hand, the paper, with the weight of his days, in the other moving hand. Then Rogovin moved into a narrow green corridor, and the line moved, and I moved up to the scales, and onto them and off, and into the green-walled hall where a line moved slowly towards a room that generated clicks and echoes of steel, the bellow of an outraged mouth.

The big Negro stood next to a tank that had glass doors on it and knobs, levers that looked cocked. 'Card to me, chin on the face-rest, chest against the lens.'

'I don't think I know the card –'

'Yellow card, I.B.M., X-ray,' he said. 'Move it up.'

I said, 'I don't think I have that one, could you. Ah. Could I check on that one? Sir?'

'Move,' he said, pulled the envelope from my hand, rammed his hand through its mouth, slapped the envelope against my chest, pounded a yellow card on top of the barrel, pushed me at a platform, pulled a lever and, when the barrel clicked, called, 'Chin on the rest, chest on the lens' and froze, waiting.

I pushed my face at the top of the machine, then closed my eyes and said, 'I got it,' and moved away at a darkened door, leaving behind a clack and hoisting, bellow, and a fluoroscope of my hand crushing a cylinder of envelope, manila, brown.

And then I was not colourblind, saw seventy-nine in green on a yellow ground, and thanked the sailor slipping slides through the vision machine in the lightless room, said 'Sir' when he told me out another door. And then I was not waxy of the ears nor swollen of the throat, and, when the doctor in the green cubicle turned his flashlight off and moved my lower jaw to close my mouth, I told him, 'Thank you, sir.' I lost my group and held my envelope and swung my sock from door to door. I saw underpants greyed with filth and yellow, rags held on by tensionless elastic, saw a tall boy, eyes as proud as a big bird's, march the floors from verdict to verdict in a union suit of white wool.

There were too many voices for hearing, then, and too many sounds for alarm. I went at doors and doctors with a glaze of dark-green wall paint layered on my eyes and the horseradish smell of bodies jumping in my sinuses. The floor got hot, or my feet grew number, I grew concerned for a poor score in blood pressure, went where a pointing finger said.

And then, my form grown reddened, the numbers of my waiting circled by the white-sleeve hands, I moved from silence to the hiss of boiling and a smell of something very very old. I came around a corner to a high-walled room with stone-topped table and a trough, a handsome soldier and a line of smiling boys. The trough was hissing, soldier shouting high and keen, 'You remove a bottle from that pile over there and you take it to that sink over there and you piss. Yeah, it's very ha-ha, it's very funny, but you better piss and piss fast because I am not gonna sit here all day and wait for you to work one up. Get the fucking *piss* up. *Move.*'

I carried a bottle to the trough and squared my shoulders, listened to the spigots in the trough hiss, closed my eyes, stopped breathing, then began again and felt warm. And then I stared ahead and heard the crooning of Rogovin: 'Oh you humper Jesus Christ come on come on come on for piss-off sakes for hump-off rubbing blue-wick oh come on come on come on.' He crouched at the wide and crowded sink, his head aimed towards the high ceiling, fat knees pushing at the trough's rough rim: 'Come on come on come on come on come on.'

I carried my hot bottle to the stone desk and watched the handsome soldier dip a strip of paper in, drop it on a towel and look away. 'You wash that bottle out clean,' he said. 'You stack it neatly when it's clean and then you take *off*.'

I washed and stacked, then walked back to bulbous Rogovin, fountain gargoyle waiting but gone dry. I said, 'Good-bye, Rogovin, I'm going home. Good-bye. Go win the war.' The trough hissed, the soldier called, the lubricated patients piddled.

He said, 'Come on come on come on come on,' and I walked along the line, sock swinging, to the doorway of the last room. ('Come on come on come on.') I squatted, and wrenched and stooped and knelt while the tape recorder chanted and a doctor watched and then I walked like a soldier, marching, swinging my arms and pounding my heels, to the shelved window and Duffy and a room of silent boys who waited to get weighed and naked.

I walked down marble steps that twined around an elevator falling, *ratchet*, rising, *ratchet*, and walked to Broadway with a U.S.A.F.E.E.S. ticket for a meal in my hand. I carried the green card to Broadway and Fulton, past newspaper stands and large amputated men on leather pads and men in gaberdine leather stores, down Fulton, then in to where the guts of television lay in bleached crates for casual picking-through by men who wore no ties, no gaberdine, and then down stairs again, away from a hint of Hudson behind the leaning piers, to cold concrete and trembling long tracks, women buying chewing gum from bulbed machines, the slot I dropped an army token into, and the peeled wood stile I turned to make the platform, catch the train that bumped me back, by stop, by stop, to Brooklyn where you yawned and lit the coffee up and asked me if I had to go away.

I told you no. I told you maybe. By the rung wide bed I told you, *ratchet*, going *ratchet*, going *ratchet*, that I mark my time by you. I tell you now, and tell you too, asleep and sweatless, that I see the high cuffs and pointed shoes of Rogovin, his fat not thick enough on marble steps in Grand Central Station as he pants down graceless to the long floor, cold tunnels, the trains that go to warm counties where the beds are single, silent, numbered, set in lines.

I think again tonight of Rogovin and tell your sleep the appetite I fed while water hissed and smells of boiling stood as stiff as Rogovin who, swollen by his own poisons, held by them, gulled by the mysteries of tissue, called 'Come on come on come on come on come on.'

I say 'Good night. Rogovin: so long. Go win the war.' And then I tell you in your sleep how I am here, and how, in winter, with my sock aloft, I struck, rode home beneath the ground.

Frederick Busch

Breathing Trouble

I

'Do you understand,' my brother said, 'that I am being squeezed to death by calories. Another bite and my breathing stops.' He pushed at the three-pound ham, pink and raw, covered with jellied broth and shining in our cabin brightly as the plastic wrap around the bread, brightly as the gold of Gulden's mustard, brightly as the stainless steel and china that were spread before him in a widening crescent like a pattern of explosion caught and kept. 'Give me enough time, the heart will harden up and turn off-yellow and fall into my stomach and break me in half. Man, thirty years old, crushed by own heart. Too much fat too soon, say M.D.s. Secretary of Health promises statement soon. The nation waits. Man –'

'You're not that fat,' I told him.

'Five-eight, two hundred and ten?'

'You weighed yourself? We don't have a scale, how could you weigh yourself? You couldn't of weighed yourself, you're guessing.'

'In the Utica Greyhound station, when I picked you up. So I weigh more now.'

'You weighed two-ten?'

'No less.'

'Well you have a very big *build* you know.'

'No doubt I'm a heavy-boned person.'

'It's allowed. You happen to be a heavy-boned person, why not, who cares.'

'I am a very fat thirty-year-old smiling private man.'

'You're not smiling.'

'Which leaves the fat. And thirty. And a filling fell out, which means pain. My head is rotting and my heart is falling down. How do you like your vacation so far?' I was up and at the icebox, getting quarts of ale, dropping caps in the long trough sink, its enamel pitted and coarse and catching blacknesses. I put the ale in front of him and went back to the hairy armchair across the room; it smelled of mildew, like the wide uneven floorboards and the low and rippling plaster ceiling, like the walls that were covered with peeling paper – two brown stallions rearing, penises sly smudged lumps, the figures repeated around and around the low little room, our whole house – and there was mildew on the mattress of my cot and his, mildew on the pinewood bookshelves, book-less and choked with clothing and cans, mildew in my nose and on his hair, and on the moist cracking oak veneer of the table where he sat before his food and said again 'How's the vacation? How do you like it? Thank you for the ale.'

'Well there's this smell' I told him. 'This kind of sneaky vinegar dirty smell.'

'It's a plant pathology. You look, say, under the table, in cracks, you see the stuff. Like cotton. Yeah, you have to grow with it for awhile, it's not an impossible thing.'

'What the *hell* are you doing looking under tables?'

'*Looking*. When you hit my age bracket there is a great deal of getting down and looking under tables to be done. It's a thing you do, you'll see.'

'You mean you been crawling around here lushing yourself up for a couple of months.'

'Refuted, brother, charge denied. While of course I have swilled some here and there and here and there, and I will admit – to you alone – to the odd stagger and occasional reel, I am only your average mild boozer. Uh-uh, no: this is a proteinhead you're dealing with, sweetmeat-stuffer. And rotter of teeth. Uh-uh twice. No sir. I am not a problem drinker.'

'You're a fucking problem *liver*' I said.

And he said 'Yes.'

So there we were, sleepy on ale and breathing in mildew, falling away into chilly shadows as twigs, then trees, and then the round green hill behind us got in the way of the sun. We were moving around and sitting, tripping over bottles and sneakers and socks, scratching, talking, sitting in silence and moving for ale, sitting, falling deeper into shadows as the Coleman lantern burned its little white cocoon and we watched it as much as we watched ourselves.

I put on a sweater and wound my watch. He pulled a wide thick shiny book from his suitcase and set it on the sticky table like a thing of glass. We did not talk then, and I heard his heavy nasal breathing as he turned the coated pages, glossy in the white light that died before it reached me. The windows were black then, I could not see out. I could not hear the insects or the shifting of brush, I could not hear a wind. I heard him breathe and heard the pages turn, I watched his thick face dip and rise and dip and rise again in the centre of the light – so bright that a gleam from the glossy pages ran on his face, as if he kneeled above a creek and the sun were rippling on his eyes. But he dipped his head above a book and the light it caught was caught on his flesh, and the windows were black, I could not hear the trees blown.

And then he said 'Hey.'

'What's the word?' I said.

'You know I went to school in nineteen fifty-five? I got

out in fifty-nine. Did you know that? You want more ale?'

'We drank it all.'

'There's whisky.'

'Later.'

'Later. So what do you think of nineteen fifty-nine?'

'Jesus. They didn't have astronauts, by gosh. I'm really stunned.'

'Well it seems like a hell of a long time ago to be a kid' he said.

'Some of my best friends are kids.'

'You're no kid, for chrissakes. You're my brother.'

'Then take my good word on this little matter: don't sweat nineteen fifty-nine.'

'Don't sweat it.'

'Let it go.'

'Blow away.'

'Roll down the calendar burial mound and seep inside of the earth.'

'Just disappear.'

'Be eaten by the teeth of time and gobbled away.'

'My god.'

'You're right, it deserves a repeat: be eaten by the tooth of time.'

'So just don't sweat old nineteen fifty-nine. It was *teeth* you said, not tooth.'

'It's what the man say.'

'What the man *know*?'

'What you mean, man?'

'*You* the mean man.'

'How that?'

'This.' He held up the heavy book, resting his elbows on the tacky table as if the book might fall. 'Nineteen fifty-nine. The class of nineteen fifty-nine. They left out Marshall and they left out me. Who's gonna know what I look like ten years down the pipe? Listen, man: I am a very melancholy graduate. That's sad to be.'

'Marshall,' I said.

'Marshall Destey.' He was pointing at the book, he said 'They left our pictures out. Marshall Destey and me. They put us in Camera Shy. God.'

'Marshall would be –'

'Crazy person. College friend of the formative years. Graveyard chum. I mean Marshall was my *skull.*' He pushed at the food again and looked to his right. There was nothing to his right except the icebox and the sink. They were in darkness. 'We didn't have the two bucks in our senior year when they took the pictures, so we refused on principle to have our pictures made. I don't know. *I* didn't have the money, it was Marshall refused on principle I guess. He had principles up the ass he didn't even know about, he had so many. I was only broke, I *couldn't* have the picture shot. Later on I got the principle. They put us both in Camera Shy. We got together, just you can't quite see us there. How's the old vacation?'

By this time I was out of the range of the lantern and back again and the bourbon was poured and he was drinking. I was back in the chair and drinking too – slowly, letting the edges of a mouthful down my throat as if the bourbon were thick, or as if it tasted good. 'It's a real expensive vacation with bourbon like this' I said.

'You don't mind being here. I mean you don't feel silly coming out here with the old runaway and listening to this and everything.'

'Come on. It's *you.*'

'Well I don't see you study any incredible amounts terribly much.'

'I'll study.'

'Don't you have exams after Easter?'

'I'll study.'

'I mean it's okay with me. You know. Just I don't want to bust up school for you. You know? You understand?'

'I'll study, Joe. Don't fret books. Can I talk about Connie?'

He held the top of the tumbler and his hand was an insect, frightened and white, waiting. He said, 'She's your sister.'

'In-law.'

'Law.'

'I mean sister-in-law.'

'That's right.'

'You want to talk about her?'

'I thought you wanted to talk about her. I was talking about Destey.'

'Easy, Cisco.'

'Easy. What the hell. Sure. Yeah, why don't we talk about Connie if you want. Why not.'

'It's only I saw her at the house before I came up.'

The hand didn't move. I kept my eyes on the hand. 'She's okay' he said.

'Well.'

'She's got enough bread.'

'Yes.'

'The kid's okay.'

'Sure. He's fine.'

'She knows I'm coming back.'

'She says there was this conversation about getting old. Middle-aged.'

'Doesnt she?'

'Connie says you were feeling, ah – desperate she says. So she doesn't really –'

'Now she *knows* I intend to come back.'

'She mentioned something about the crib?'

'The kid wasn't in it.'

'That's why she isn't so sure.'

'Man. Look, I hit the crib. I put my fist through the crib, but the kid wasn't in it, he was on the table, I was changing him.'

'I think she got scared.'

'Sure she got scared. Listen: *I* got scared. I mean he was there screaming, out of the back of his throat, like the *skin* was peeling off. God. And my neck kept swelling up, tighter and tighter and tighter, I couldn't move my head. Bam. Like that, right through the plywood. And of course I started to cry. Like a goddam kid if you will excuse the expression. The two of us, him screaming and me kind of chugging around in my throat, I kept saying Shush, Shush. And Connie came in and the whole fucking roof went off the house.'

'She mentioned that. You said some things –'

'I said This is no way to be a free man. I said I'm dying here, I'm an old man. She told me to take it easy and she was like a street dog with a stranger, her eyes were all big, scared to come over across the room. So I said some things and I went over to the studio and I was shaking so much I couldn't pick my teeth much less get work done. You know, so I tried to just do busywork, just kill time, and I couldn't do that? I couldn't of swatted the biggest fat fly if it had infantile paralysis on the *floor* for chrissakes. I went back and I said some things and I took off.'

'She told me.'

'So you said.'

'I'm sorry. I think we could skip this.'

'Not if you want to talk.'

'Later maybe.'

'Now, kid. You want to talk, we talk.'

'Well I don't know what to *say*. I don't think you're old.'

'Now come on.'

'And I think the baby is fine. Connie's a terrific woman, Joey. She's beautiful.'

'Now. Come on.'

'And I was always having these thoughts of all three of you, man. I don't want to get in your way, Joey. You know: I don't want to shove. I just always was thinking about you and Connie and your baby. I'm sorry.' My hand was over my eyes and my eyes were shut and my hand shook.

Joey said 'Now.' He said, 'Come on.'

I said, 'Apologies. We could maybe talk about this later on.'

'Why not?'

'When I don't get on your ass.'

'I'm a little bit your property' he said. 'You can talk.'

'Later.'

'Later.' I rubbed at my eyes and then I looked across the darkness of the cold room and into the white light and there was his hand, poised on the glass, and I could not see his hand move though the bourbon shimmered and caught light and threw it out. 'You could tell me something else about Destey' I said, straight and even, dull.

'Amazing man' he said. 'He always wore a bowler hat, one of those tiny-brim roundtop jobs. It was too small on him so he wore it perched, the hat was always falling off. He drank quarts of beer in a graveyard. I mean this is innocent stuff. Just beer. And a graveyard across the street from a bar. Beer and tombstones, like a movie, silly shit.' The door clanged, it was like a heavy bell. Joey's hand went straight, flat above the glass and the sound of the beaten door went ringing in the room. 'Nobody comes here' he said.

'I didn't even tell her what city I was going to.'

'She wouldn't come. She knows I'm coming home.'

'She doesn't, Joey. She has fears.'

He was standing, almost, crouched above the debris of his appetites, face gone white in the light of the lantern, white with black shadow hollows at the eyes and mouth. 'Well me too, buddy. So do I.'

And then the door swung in and a little kid in a bright red poplin jacket, wire-rimmed glasses on his round white face, said, 'Grandma.'

And Joey said 'Oh no. Not me, I'm not.'

2

So we were being beaten by brush, the three of us, Joey and me and the kid who could not catch his breath, crushing through high wet grass and low branches, looking for grandma and passing the bourbon back and forth over the little guy's head.

Then Joey was ahead of me, he had the bottle with him, and I stared at his long yellow slicker as his voice came back: 'So tell me how you lose a grandma.'

I called up 'Joe, he can't breathe, we have to stop. Hey? Joey? Stop here awhile, okay?'

The slicker came back at us in the darkness and Joey said 'And while you're telling, you can tell me how the woods get wet when it doesn't rain.'

He was right, there was moisture coming off the low branches like thick sap squeezed up, and a tree felt sticky when a hand pushed off it or scrabbled with nails for support. The stones we slipped on were clammy; grass and moss, lichen, fern, they all were puffy with a moisture so heavy and slow to run that the flesh between the fingers leeched the fingers stuck as if a syrup or a clotting blood were clinging and coating and would not wipe off. We'd started in blackness as pure as the ring in our room around the lantern, but a shelf of clouds above the trees that bound us in had lifted off and, as I lay with my head on a rock, my body soaking the moisture that poured up from the earth, I saw the low-toned yellow light behind the clouds go on as if a tide were sweeping the sky. We were in greyness, there was half-light everywhere, and clouds too high to touch came dropping, promising soon to touch us where we lay.

No nightbird sang. The woods were thick around us, and what the boy called trail was tough grass, a green wet wiry fibre that sprang up behind us as we moved: we had not passed. Winds came off or around the high round hill against which Joey's cabin sat. But the cabin was gone, the hill was lost in back of hidden contours we had run, and there were just the slimy trees, the stones, the dropping sky, Joey in his slicker bobbing his head and tonguing the mouth of the bottle of bourbon, and the little boy panting, a steadiness of sound from invisible insects, root-deep smell of rich wet earth and anything that lived in it and, in the slippery trees, an absence of song.

'I have this trouble breathing' the boy said. He squatted like an Indian at my side, panting very deeply, a wet thick grinding in his throat and upper chest as if there were a fat black something in its glistening throes that called from him to us. He rubbed his palms on his dungarees, rubbed, rubbed, and his little face collapsed and expanded while he tried to smile, his flesh was trying to breathe.

He stood, quickly, and rubbed his palms on his little chest. 'What is that?' I said. 'You need help?'

'I get this asthma sometimes. It goes away. When I get excited sometimes I have this breathing trouble.' The glasses were on me square and I looked at Joey. He looked at me. The little boy panted, and then a high keen sound came out of his throat, a distant whistle, dying. He shook his head fast, he smiled, his face collapsed and expanded as he said 'It's okay. It just *does* that, don't worry.'

So when I stood up and put my hands on his shoulders I said 'Well what the hell, why should I worry? I used to have that too. It goes away. When you grow up. It does. Meanwhile, when I was your age–'

'I'm nine. I'll be ten October twenty-fifth.'

'Yeah, right, I was nine, ten, eleven, I used to go out to my grandma's in the country, it would really help, being out in the country and everything.' I looked at Joey when the boy moved in, and he kept his eyes on me when the boy fell onto my waist and his hands held on and his face in my diaphragm rocked while he sobbed and while his weeping turned to grunted grabs for air. I rubbed his back and looked at Joe. The high long whistle came and Joe put the bottle in the pocket of his yellow slicker and stood and watched.

Joey said 'Okay. Now. We have to know your name.'

The head moved.

'Because we all have to help each other now. So tell us your name.'

His head moved, his arms stayed on my waist, and his voice, in the wool of my hunting jacket, came up. 'Jordan. My name is Jordan. Grandma ran away.'

'Why did she go?' Joey said. 'Was she drunk?'

Jordan dropped off me and turned around and then he leaned against me as a scared man, fighting, leans against a wall. I was no wall, I felt his body seize for air. He said 'Grandma doesn't get drunk.'

And Joey smiled. He nodded his head and he smiled and he said 'I apologize. Just you try to find the simplest answers first, you understand? I hope you forgive me.'

'Grandma doesn't drink liquor,' Jordan said.

'I take it back' Joey said. He nodded, he smiled, he looked at the ground. 'I take it back.'

I said 'Was she sick? Did your grandma have asthma? Was she feeling sick?'

His head moved against me, up and down, and Joey said 'What with? What'd she have?'

'Oldness,' Jordan said.

I said, 'That's what she told you? Just that?'

'Oldness,' Jordan said.

Joey said, 'Well that's enough.'

The whistle rose and I rubbed at Jordan's neck. I asked him 'Did she tell you anything else?'

'She told me I should finish my supper and she would go outside and she would be right back in. She put on the sweater that I gave her. My mom bought it but I gave it. For Christmas. And she went outside and she didn't come home. So I went out later on and I found you but I didn't find her.'

'Did you call your Mom?'

'We don't have a telephone. Grandma I mean. She doesn't have a telephone. My mom's not home. She's driving my father to the army. He's a captain in Vietnam. They have to go to Carolina, in the south.'

'So we're doing a job for the military-industrial-familial complex' Joey said. 'They come and get you, don't they' he said. 'All you have to do is wait.'

'Well we have to find Jordan's grandma' I said.

Joey said 'We'll find her. I guarantee. No doubt. She's looking for us. She never even heard of us and maybe she's in another county by now, but she will find us. Rest, and be assured.'

'Joey.'

'Brother,' he said, 'that was only words. I'm a big fat rotten buzzard losing teeth, and those are the words I can sing. But we move on now. Here we go. A little hide and seek. We'll go to Jordan's house and look around and start from there. We'll find her. She'll find us. All will be found. Or not.'

We took off, then, Jordan – his little breaths, his gulping tries, the high thin mucous scream inside his chest – holding my hand very tightly, and Joey, wide and wobbling in his shiny slicker, raging behind us and snapping wood and crushing leaf, thudding too fast for the shape he was in and paying for it quickly, quickly beginning to pant in the hollows of his rich flesh. I listened to Jordan, I listened to Joey, I paced my crooked steps to what their breathing was, and so we ran in grey light, the moist near-darkness, to the rhythms that their sobbing sang.

3

In Sheridan's Bar in Utica, New York: The bus that stopped across the street is gone and I am here, heavy suitcase heavier with the heaviest of books, and here is Joey, leading me to the windowless wall and through the door – there is a footmat on the floor, and it says S – into the smell of phlegm and sawdust that is Sheridan's. There is a wall to our right, covered with metal plates stamped S and painted over ochre, and it runs the length of the short narrow room. You can walk on either side of the wall, there's a door in the middle, it opens into and out of the bar; the corridor on the other side is there for the sake of the door; the door exists for the wall; the lighting is bad and the bar is very dark. I follow Joey's wobbling ass and watch the haunches slither as he slides up onto a stool, I sit beside him and I grin. I want to put my forehead on his shoulder and I grin.

The counter is damp and sticky, sudsy drained glasses are pushed away from the counter's cornice up and down the bar. We are alone in Sheridan's backed by the wall and fronted by a mirror, fogged with winds that blow in Sheridan's and blocked by dainty designs – the one chunked upon another with a trembling hand perhaps unused to helping things to not fall down – in quarts of port and muscatel. The cash register is ninety years old, it is where the men of Sheridan's have signed their softest names, leaving, leaving. I look at my brother, I grin to him and then we both smile. His fingers drum on the bar.

'Hymie,' he says, 'this is my brother.' Hymie is a roundness of rumpled white with red hands and red face, a nose that melts while we watch into red lines and blue shadows, he is a bruise. He nods and extends the nod to a dip and purses his lips and spits on the floor behind the bar. He wipes his mouth with the bar rag he carries around his neck, he wipes the bar with the rag. 'Two of your cleanest draughts, please, Hymie' my brother says.

I say 'Maybe we should stick to grass.'

Joey says 'I'm off it. I don't do it anymore.'

'I've got enough, I'll leave you some.'

'No, no. I have forsworn the toke for the rest of my days. I refuse to cloud my perceptions. Except with bourbon. I go *swimming* in that.'

Hymie spits and puts the beers down, takes Joe's money and, when the register sings, a voice comes up from the end of the L of the bar, in darkness, where the window on the street in Utica should be: 'I can't see Porter. Can you? You can't see him. We couldn't get to him poor Porter he's down.' In the shadows he has no face, he has shadows twisted and ropey on his crewcut head. He has eyes and sinuous shadows, and the eyes are red as his tumbler of muscatel, his wine is red as blood. 'Porter he's down at the bottom we couldn't get him out. Poor Porter. Poor Porter. Fargh olie olie don the calendar. All of the time. *Ah!* Down on the calendar I can't prove it. Can you? Can you? Two men came in they had on shirts. Can you prove *that*?'

I look at Joey and his eyes are closed. The change for a five is piled beside his beer, and he pushes the beer away, he pushes away the change, he says to Hymie 'This is for my other relative down at the end of the bar.' He pushes off the stool, his eyes are closed, he is holding onto my arm, and Hymie seizes the money, spits.

In a 1965 Ford Falcon: Joey says 'How are you doing in school?'

I say 'I think the school is doing me.'

He says 'Well we are all getting done now, aren't we?'

'I don't think it's that bad. I mean it's *bad*, but there's no fear, you know. Nothing fearful. I can survive.'

'I don't think I can.' He laughs from his throat and starts the car, it grinds, grinds. 'Or maybe. I don't know. I never didn't know, it's a problem in itself.'

'I hope you do.'

'What?'

'Survive.' He laughs from his throat and it sounds like skin is peeling off inside. I think of blood the colour of cheap and watery wine. I say 'Well I think you should. I hope you do. I really think you should.' He laughs from his throat. I close my eyes.

In the grass behind his shack: He is naked on a blanket when I come out, he is covered in sun and the snorts and chuffings of creatures in the brush, hummings of bugs, birdshriek. The skin is yellowed, the fatty pelvic girdle and long thick penis, dark in the dark groin hair, are stunning to see,

I am a child on the edge of adolescence, easy and naked with his father for the last time, knowing already a sense of end. He puts his palms down flat beside him, rocks his great buttocks and thighs into air and holds them – toneless muscle vertical, pods of flesh fed past flesh's need – and farts a long and greasy bubbling shout of his innards to me. I turn and cock a leg at him and grunt and say my organs back. And his voice comes out from behind the shaky healthless skin: 'You can't prove *that.*'

In the shack at noon: Joey smears the mayonnaise across the pulpiness of white bread. The wrapping says the bread is fresher since it has no holes, is not permitted in the factory to have holes. He is watching the knife go over the bread, then watching the fork as it lifts up the soft compressed tuna from the can and, dripping clear bubbly heavy oil, crushes the fish in soft furrows of the mayonnaise. He finishes making the sandwich and swallows his saliva and says 'This is really Miracle Whip. I don't like mayo as much as this.' He doesn't look at me. He wipes his fingers on his pants, picks up the sandwich, squeezes the soft bread – there is oil on his fingers again, clear thick oil on the backs of his hands – and eases a corner of sandwich into his mouth. He doesn't look at me. He chews and breathes deeply, settles his buttocks, plants his forearms again on the table – oil is on his wrists, lightly – and then he stops. He very slowly puts the sandwich down, pushes his rounding stomach at the table's edge to hold a crumb of tuna held to bread by the shiny white paste. He captures the crumb and puts it in his mouth. He picks up his sandwich. His eyes disappear. And I have disappeared to him. He has no eyes. There is oil on his forearm. A fly whines nastiness high on a wall and goes in six directions at the mildewed stallions but the fly is going only one way, really, it is coming to crouch.

In bed at night in darkness: 'How does your garden grow?' he says. 'I mean how *are* you. Really how.'

I sniff at the tang of mildew and listen to an owl. I watch what creeps across my closed-off sight behind the shapes that scatter underneath my bony lids. 'I'm good' I say. 'I'm happy I'm here.'

'Yeah. Well I am too.'

'Me too.'

'That's right.'

'I hope that things –'

'That's right.'

I listen to the owl awhile and then I say 'I like the way that bird goes on.'

'I'm glad you came' he says.

'I know.'

'I know.'

4

And we stood at the door of the house. Jordan stopped, then he went on and we waited, at the paintless grey-wood house that was shaped like a barn with many windows and a small set of steps that didn't any longer touch the sill they climbed to. The trees were close in, they touched the house, they came down low and green and heavy with moisture and swept at the roof and raked with a sound of stone on stone the flat coarse sides of grey board that dust and wind and water were smoothing. The gold-grey light was bright there, and the house was phosphorescent, something in the wood replied to weather. Only the windows didn't glow; they were the visionless eyes of an animal dead and staring, still and calm and blind. And then the flashlight jumped and wavered and a window glowed, went out, as Jordan – I could feel him reach for air, I heard his lungs moan – went from room to room, looking. Joey and I were in the high wet grass, clammy and panting, waiting for Jordan, Joey in the yellow slicker, leaving the bottle where it was. And Joey talked.

'I was a cripple' he said. 'Well I wasn't really, I was hurt. I was almost hurt. It was some kind of exam-time, I don't remember, and I couldn't study, so I played basketball at the outdoor courts all goddam night it felt like for about a week. Being a totally non-athletic athlete – lots of sweat and great willingness to play dirty and very little skill. You know?' I shuffled my feet and nodded but he didn't see. 'So some huge professional Lutheran athlete with a crew-cut came down on me off a rebound and I went down and almost sprained my ankle, but that was good enough. Next scene: me in my dormitory room, alone, in a wheelchair, naturally unable to study on account of the pain I did not have, sweating, touching at a textbook that scared me, you know what I mean.' I didn't bother to nod.

'In comes Destey, very short, skinny, he's wearing his bowler hat and blue jeans, high white sneakers. The costume. Little round face and big glasses. Waiting for me to say hello. So I say Hello Destey, something like that.

'And he just stares. I remember how yellow his teeth were, bad yellow. The door to my room was open and the hallway was painted college hallway green and in the light from the hallway *he* looked yellow. Very bad. So I say Hello again or How'd you like to buy me some beer? Something like that. And he just looks.

'Then he hoists up his little skinny arm and he has a plastic vial. He says "How would you like to tell me why I shouldn't take these? How'd you like to give me some reasons?"

'So I say something totally unfunny like "Wrong prescription".

'And he says, "*Tell* me!" And I begin to sweat, I don't know what to say. He looks at me and *whoosh,* he's gone, like he had a cape whipping behind him, the door is slammed and he's gone. I sit there like a jerk and all of a sudden I think, you know, he *means* it, he sure as hell means something, and I am limping out the door as if it hurts. It doesn't hurt. I start thinking of reasons to give him.

'It was so much like a *movie*! Me limping over the quadrangle at some absurd time of night and Destey – I just catch a shot of him – low over the ground, moving towards the chapel. You know what it looks like, all high and huge and gothic. It's a goddam *night*mare, they could scare you into loving Jesus Christ with that. So there he is, crouching in and out of the campus lights, black-green ground all over the place, and me limping after him. He disappears.

'The chapel is black inside, there are only the altar lights, all the way up this wide stone aisle, flagstone, everything clicks when you move on it in there. And there is this *huge* ceiling, it's so high and heavy, the place wasn't meant for people. And all that stone is cold to touch, man. And there's Destey. Tiny. Growling like an animal up at the altar, sunk in behind the lectern, snarling and spitting on the red rug, laughing like a villain in a movie who mostly means his part. He's up there hammering on things, I hear wood and metal beating all the hell over the place, he's kicking at baseboard, tearing pages out of the Bible. I mean he is on his *way*.

'So I say something persuasive like Come on down, Destey and he looks out and shouts "Hello, Joey., don't bother me."

'I tell him we're not allowed in the church after ten o'clock at night and he tells me to bug off. He says "Take your injury and your fat ass and go outside." I say some other things and he looks at the lectern and then he looks up and he gives his little sermon. It was *nuts*! "Chil-dren," he screams. "Children. My children, nobody *knows* anymore. No-oo. Nobody *knows* how they cry except me. Nobody *knows* how it cries, but I do, I. Do. So. *Yes*! I know. I *know*!"'

And then Joey was silent, we looked at each other and listened to his words pound off the side of the house. I watched him listen to his breath, and I heard the language of Destey's lament ring on golden organ pipes high in their loft, ring down to wooden pews, hang heavy in thin air along the cold granite walls where my brother was less heavy with his appetites and still expecting to be glad.

He took a breath and he began again. 'He shouts "Joey! Go away! *Please*! Can't you leave me alone? Please?" Then he turns around to this enormous crucifix behind him and he hits his fists against his little legs, over and over, keeps hitting, he *moans*: "You stupid bastard, you cheap queer, soap-suds, piss – white-chested fairy bastard Jew! Can't you get the hell. To think. To think. That I. To think. To think."

'He stops and he stands there and he's so fucking made of *skin* in there – maroons and ambers, the shiny wood of the altar, woollen rugs and silk flags and gold. He keeps his fists against his thighs and shuffles like he's a toy over to a stack of collection bowls. Really. Like a toy.' Jordan stood at the steps of the house. He shook his head and put a white plastic inhalator in his mouth and pressed it and breathed. The inhalator made the sound of someone choking. Jordan pressed, breathed, walked slowly over with big eyes blurred behind his glasses, looked at Joey and shook his head. I put my arm around his neck and he moved in and he stayed there, pressing out a noise of choking and breathing in to kill the whistling of his lungs. 'And he starts in throwing them – onto the floor, into the close pews, in the air, at the organ pipes, up at those goddam simpering stained-glass windows which he could never hit. He keeps saying "Uh" and throwing, then saying "Uh" and throwing again, over and over until the bowls are gone and I can't hear them bouncing anyplace. I hear him breathing and I see the light catch on his glasses and I see his yellow teeth and then he pushes and pushes and pushes and this huge high lectern goes over like a tree. Like a tree. I cover my ears and I go down on one knee like a scared kid. I'm telling you. They could *scare* you into Christ in there. He's shaking up there, and he looks down the church and runs out the minister's door and slams out of the church. Am I rocking on my ass?

'But I catch up in some fraternity parking lot. He's waiting for me, he looks like he's waiting. I stand still, and he stands still and he says "Before me lie deserts of vast eternit-ie."

'I say "Oh bullshit, Destey" and move towards him. Then I stop. Then I go in again and I'm bending and pulling and levering and we're rolling all over the grass and gravel and his breath stinks like vomit, horrible. I get my arms around him and I squeeze him into me. The old fearful hug of the bear. I get my face into his whiskers and of course we're both lying there on the ground at the edge of the campus, hugging each other and crying like a couple of scared kids. Something. I don't know.'

Jordan stared at Joey, his mouth was an O around the plastic, and he stared without moving. Joey put his hands in the pockets of his slicker and looked at me, looked away at the low wet leafage, in grey-gold light, then back at me. 'Well she didn't come home' he said.

'Jordan says no.'

'There's a car around the back of the house, I see its ass-end sticking out. There are tracks from the tyres, see?

You're with Natty Whosit, King of the Deer. We'll take the car.'

'Where are we going?' Jordan said. His arm was around my waist, he was holding us together. 'I don't know where to go.'

'We'll get in the car and I'll show you where to go' Joey said. 'This is my reservation here. I'll show you a very secondary road and I'll show you where she is. I have some worries about it. But we'll go. I know where grandma is. Where else?'

5

I sat in the back of the Volkswagen and kept a hand on Jordan's head. I was shivering, and I waited for a hint of cold, but the heater was on and we were humping ruts and scraping branches, lurching hard, and sweat was under my arms and in my crotch.

The engine was wet, it giggled little explosions. I called over the bursts and stutterings 'What'd Destey do?' In the dark cockpit of the back there was a sweetness of apples and then the bite of corruption, garbage pit and orchard both, at once. On the floor several cores rolled as the car stammered with its yellow lights at the blank grey face of the country. The cores were nibbled closely, jagged from teeth. And in the dead and drying yellowed pulp, under threads and debris that they had attracted and kept, were the seeds. They were brown and hard and locked. They rolled around and the angry sweet decay came up. I said 'Destey. What'd he do?' Jordan made the squeezing sound and leaned to my hand. 'Joey? What'd he decide to do with himself? Huh? What'd he decide to do?'

Joey was low on the wheel, swinging the wheel, driving with no accuracy at all, yet curving when the slim road curved, leaning into curves before they came, straightening the arc before I saw that the rutted rocky road was going to be straight. Still, the car wobbled and spun off big rocks, clanked on trees, he was breaking the car apart, he almost had no control, but he knew where to go, he was going there. And Jordan pumped away and leaned to my hand as Joey busted us up and leaned to the narrow road. 'Bowie knife stuck into his headboard. Rope in a hangman's noose tied to a light-cord. Pills all over the bureau. Beer all night in the goddam cemetery like somebody had a camera turned on. He never talked to me again, purely refused.'

I saw a small woman in a cheap wool sweater, sockless feet in the work shoes of a man. She stood and she lifted a hand and she dropped it and she walked towards me. Her face was smooth, hair as grey as soft steel wool, and she stared in my eyes and walked towards me and disappeared.

'He got into some girl's car and got himself all drunked up and beat the car to death in the countryside and ploughed it into a tree. Totalled the car. Naturally. He didn't even have a licence.' Jordan's head dropped back and he breathed in gurgling wheezes, scared into sleep. The plastic gadget lay in his lap while he ran away. 'And he flunked his courses of course.'

'Of course.'

'They sent him home.'

'On crutches. Like he was coming home from a war. In his last year there.'

'What else? I heard he got a job in a camera store. Down south. In the land of dismal swamps. That's all I heard.'

'Well I guess that's enough. So what are you going to do? Joey?'

'What? You realize that you are conversing with the

driver while the vehicle's in motion. But what. What would you like to know?

'I asked you. What do you intend to do?'

'I intend to drive this car with my customary expertise.'

'I mean *what*.'

'You mean Connie.'

'Well her.'

'I intend to drive this car.'

'Okay.'

'What else am I supposed to know, compadre. What else kind of answers am I supposed to have.'

'Right.'

'Don't *right* me. You don't have to jerk me like that. You don't need to sit up on my shoulder and give me shit like *right*.'

'Okay.'

'Well what would you like me to *say*?'

'I'm sorry.'

'Well I am. I don't mind saying it to you. I am.'

'No, I mean *I* am. Really. You know it. I know what you're saying.'

'I know.'

'I'm sorry.'

'So am I. I still am.'

'So am I.'

'Both.'

'Both.'

The lady in Sears Roebuck high-ankled shoes came back, her hair was blowing, her eyes were closer, they were hollow, I saw through her sockets and her eyes were filled with the sky. He stopped the car and Jordan said 'Is this where she is? Is she here? Ooh. I'm afraid of this. I really am.'

'Joey'll find your grandma.'

'She said it was oldness.'

'I guess you could run away for that.'

'You think she was mad at me?'

Joey said 'She wasn't mad at you.' He turned the engine off and cut the lights. 'Jordan, would you stay here.'

'Where's grandma?'

He said 'We'll go find your grandma and bring her back.'

'I'm scared of this,' Jordan said. 'I don't want to stay here I don't think.' The inhalator was in his mouth, pumping. 'This is scary I think.'

Joey said 'I think.'

I said 'So we all go.' I picked up Jordan's hand and Joey got out of the car, the slicker went off to the woods to the left of the road and Jordan dropped my hand, left it hanging over the seat, as he followed. And we all went, into the pine and the ground covered with soft decaying needles and mushy turf, away from the grey half-light into blackness, and into fine slashing branches and rotten traps that pit-mounds made, the holes in the earth where moss and lichen and white wet larvae came when high old trees went down and their roots were torn up into the air. I followed the wheeze of Jordan's breath and the pump of his little machine, I followed the fading away of the yellow slicker. And every time a breathy wind picked branches up to let in grey I stopped, I studied to be certain that the grey was cloud and listless moon, and not a lady's hair.

So I was far behind them after awhile, I was alone, the slicker was gone and the sound of fast water was drumming over the sound of Jordan's breath and I stopped because I was alone. My foot crushed in a pine cone, or the pulpy skull of something small, long-dead. I saw the lady and I said 'I'm young enough to see a thing like you, I'm young enough to whistle' and I did and she was gone. My hand on a branch of pine came wet off the feathery needles and sticky with resin. When I made a fist the fist glued shut. I hit my thigh with it and hit and hit and then I pulled my fingers apart and walked. The noise of water was harsher now, and it had a bounce, a sense of echo that gave it height, a hint of dark canyon and crumbling rock and flesh peeled off on canyon walls and pieces of bone blow, luminous, white. The sound said *See your brother here. He knows the road. He has kneeled at water and wondered.* I said 'He'll die from food.' The sound said *See.* I said 'His heart will fall on his stomach' and the sound said *See.*

The noise was beating my head, wetness from the waterfall was on my face and the trees dripped, branches nodded, dripping, as the noise of water beat them like a wind. And there were no trees, there was an edge of sandy earth in grey half-light, boulders bunched high, huge round mica-shiny greynesses and thick bush and dewberry, arrowhead, teasel and cress and, at the edge, a lady, asleep. Her knees were up to her chest, her thin white legs were luminous and her feet were in high heavy shoes. Her hair was grey, she was a small shape. In the howl of water on stone and thunder of only water Jordan squeezed and squeezed the plastic machine and the sound got lost. And Joey sat a little back, sat in his yellow slicker shiny with the wetness that was every place tonight and leaned his face beneath that bottle of bourbon and looked straight up and drank, drank.

Mel Calman

The Fifty Minute Hour

The room is small. The couch supports me. The face opposite is bare like a white screen waiting for me to project myself onto it.

I see a birthday cake covered in pink candles. My sister's cake. I think of red ballet shoes. The film. Anton Walbrook. Moira Shearer.

My daughter dancing round and round in her white satin tutu. She is seven and wants to be a dancer and a nurse and an actress and a princess in her spare time.

And my sister is dead.

She wanted to be a dancer and a princess when she grew up. And own a pair of red ballet shoes.

The white screen speaks. *What are you thinking?*

Nothing.

Did I tell you my sister's dead? And my father. And my mother.

I can't eat away from home. I can't sleep without dreaming of death. I can't live without dying. I can't see because a blind man stands beside me. I am guilty of being alive.

I can't go on. I can't go back. Please doctor, can't you find someone else to be me?

What are you thinking?

Nothing.

I look at my watch. The fifty minute hour is nearly up. Riddle: When is an hour not an hour? When it's shrunk by the Head Shrinker. The Head Shrinker needs ten minutes to recover his wits between patients. Poor Shrink. Poor me. Why do I come? Ask me another riddle.

It is quiet here. The gas fire softly burns up the oxygen. I'll make an omelette for supper. Then a slow bath. Then bed. Change the sheets. White sheets. Shrouds.

The funeral was peaceful. A summer's day. We pushed the black trolley along the path and I listened carefully to the wheels on the gravel. I rested one hand on the black cloth as if gently touching her and saying: There, there. It will be all right now. Don't worry. It will be all right. I promise.

No panic. No dilemmas. Tranquillized for eternity. Try a little death. Three times a day – before meals.

It's better for you to be wheeled gently along on this black trolley than to struggle against the tide of your black fears.

What are you thinking?

Nothing.

I still have a few grains of earth under my fingernails. As we walked back from the grave, I felt the need to pull some leaves off the bushes beside the path. I crushed them in my fingers and smelt the green smell and was reassured. And later I read in the prayer book that this was the traditional action of the Jewish mourner. It is customary to pluck some grass and say: And they of the city shall flourish like the grass of the earth.

The doctor stands up. Well . . .

I sit up and look out of the window at the trees in the square. The fifty minute hour has passed away.

I walk down the stairs and shut the front door carefully so as not to disturb anyone.

I want to go back to the room and watch the gas fire and be safe.

If I survive until tomorrow and return, how can I be sure that the room will still be there?

Mel Calman

The Artist

A fresh canvas..
All I need is a
subject
worthy of it...
Something epic, of course-
But with truth, humanity,
compassion, irony,
wit, passion,
insight..

An allegory? I think not.
Something universal but not commercial
Personal but
not too private..

One mustn't rush these things...
The mood must be right..!
The ambience.. etc..
Great art takes
time to mature..

Perhaps I'm not quite ready to begin.
I ought to suffer more, meditate more,
live more
before I start.
I feel a seed germinating inside me..
If I stay very still perhaps it will grow
& grow into something
beautiful...

No!
It seems to have
aborted itself...

At last I think I see it... The creative
process is truly absorbing... The wa
the unconscious sifts one's experienc
and renders it into the true concept
of art...

Was it not Jung who said:
The artist is the mythmaker
of the tribe...

I'm ready to begin now..

Ah....

Yes!

Hello! isn't that
a dead artist?
That must be his
last work!

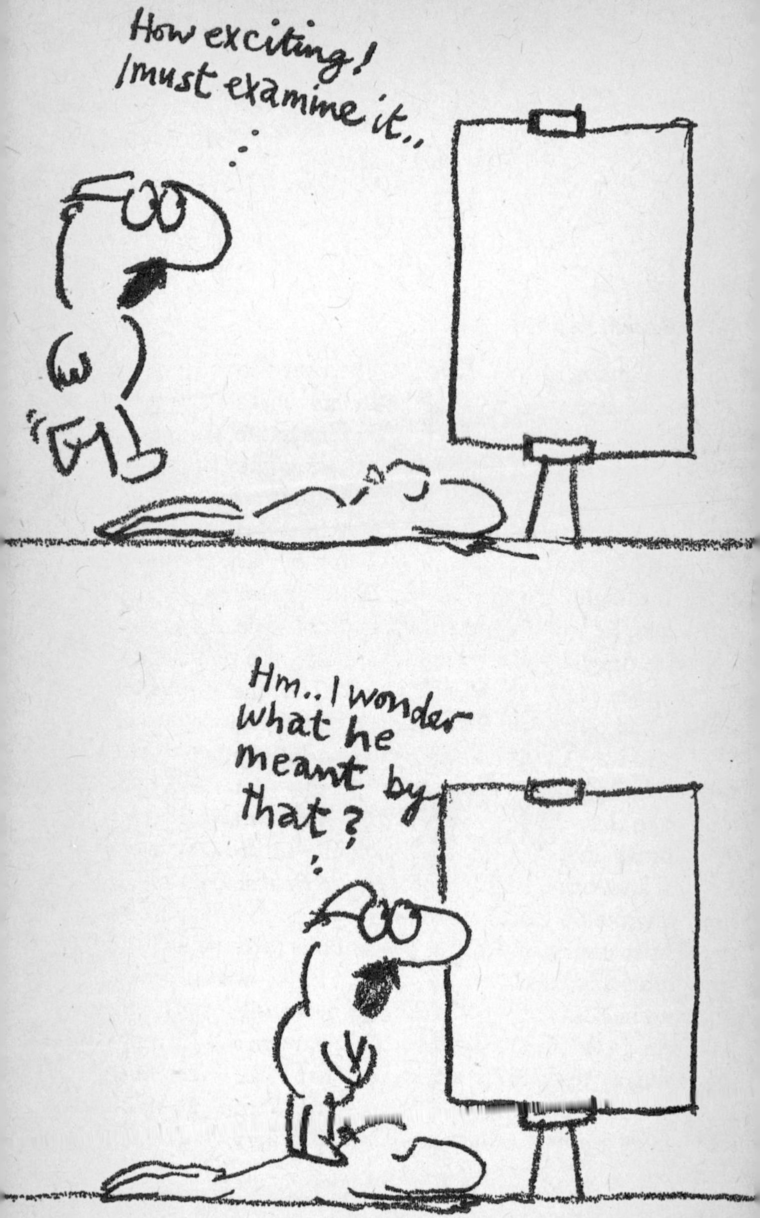

How exciting!
I must examine it..

Biographical Notes

Victor Sawdon Pritchett

born in London in 1900 has published over 200 short stories and has been described as 'the complete short story writer'. Of his early struggles, he says: 'Everyone has to work under more or less impossible circumstances when they begin, and that's a very good thing. I had the idea that to be a writer I must leave home and never go back. So I went to France and got a job in a photographer's shop in Paris, and after that, in the glue and shellac trades.' After selling glue for two years, he was commissioned to write little vignettes to illustrate drawings of bridges, and these were published in the *Christian Science Monitor*, *Time and Tide*, the *Westminster Gazette*, and other weeklies. He became a travelling essayist 'in a mild way', and feels that a certain 'foreignness of eye' is essential to the good short story writer. 'You need to be foreign to the scene,' he says, and points out that Kipling was abroad in India, that Maugham was brought up in France, and that the Irish are foreign to English culture. He himself wrote his first short story while he was in Spain as a newspaper correspondent, a job he didn't like at all, and though his first collection, *The Spanish Virgin*, was a success, he found he couldn't sell any more stories until *New Writing* paid him £3 for *The Sailor* and established him as a 'promising young writer'. 'Short stories are what I like doing best,' he says, but claims that he still has stories turned down on such trivial grounds as indecency and impropriety. He lives near Regents Park and writes every day, visiting America at intervals to lecture on the English comic tradition. Besides his seven collections of short stories, he has published five novels, four books of literary criticism, three travel books and portraits of three cities, London, Dublin and New York. The first volume of his autobiography *A Cab at the Door* was published in 1968 and gives a 'brilliantly belligerent' picture of the chaos and drama of his family life in the first years of the century.

Ruth Fainlight

was born in New York and educated in the States and in England where she spent a year at the Birmingham College of Arts and Crafts and a year at the Brighton College of Arts and Crafts. After this she had jobs as salesgirl, cashier, teacher, travel agency representative and interviewer. She began writing poetry when she was eleven, and her first collection of poems, *A Forecast, A Fable* was published in 1958. Since then she has published three more books of poems, the most recent being *To See the Matter Clearly* (Macmillan 1968), a translation from Lope de Vega, *All Citizens are Soldiers,* with her husband, Alan Sillitoe, and a volume of short stories *Daylife and Nightlife* published by André Deutsch earlier this year. She has two children and lives in Kent.

Frederick Busch

was born in Brooklyn, New York, in 1941, and educated at Muhlenberg College and Columbia University. From 1962–3 he held a Woodrow Wilson National Fellowship. He was a hack writer for a public relations news syndicate for a year, then spent a year on an educational magazine and taught in the evening school at City College in New York City for one semester where the students in Basic Business English complained to the chairman that he was teaching them how to read W. C. Williams instead of how to write requisitions for business equipment. He is now assistant professor of English at Colgate University, Hamilton, New York. Says he has 'been writing things and sending them to editors in seriousness' since he was seventeen. He has published stories in America and England, has written two novels, 'one bad and one only half bad', before *I Wanted a Year Without Fall,* which was published in England by Calder & Boyars earlier this year. He has just finished his fourth novel, which he says is his best, and has just returned from six months in a cottage near Salisbury where he stayed with his wife, Judy, and their baby son Benjamin while he worked on a volume of stories to be called *Breathing Trouble.*

Mel Calman

was born in London in 1931, studied illustration at St Martin's School of Art, and has worked as a cartoonist for the *Daily Express,* the *Sunday Telegraph,* the *Observer,* magazines, publishers, television and advertising agencies. He now draws regularly for the *Sunday Times,* and freelances in a number of directions. He has published several collections of cartoons including *Calman and Women, Boxes, Bed-Sit, The Penguin Mel Calman,* and *My God.* Recently he became involved in animated films, completed one, *The Arrow,* and is working on others. Says he has been writing secretly since he was at school but *The Fifty Minute Hour* is his first piece of fiction to be published without drawings. He lives in Bloomsbury 'not for its literary associations, but because it's within walking distance of the *Sunday Times* and I'm a very lazy man'.

Penguin Modern Stories

1* William Sansom Jean Rhys David Plante Bernard Malamud

2* John Updike Sylvia Plath Emanuel Litvinoff

3† Philip Roth Margaret Drabble Jay Neugeboren Giles Gordon

4† Sean O'Faolain Nadine Gordimer Shiva Naipaul Isaac Babel

5† Penelope Gilliat Benedict Kiely Andrew Travers Anthony Burton

6† Elizabeth Taylor Dan Jacobson Maggie Ross Robert Nye

7† Anthony Burgess Susan Hill Yehuda Amichai B. S. Johnson

8† William Trevor C. J. Driver A. L. Barker

**Not for sale in the U.S.A.*

†Not for sale in the U.S.A. or Canada